W9-AQT-466

The Case of
the
PURPLE MARK

Westminster Press Books by
CHARLES COOMBS

Celestial Space, Inc.
The Case of the Purple Mark

The Case of
the
PURPLE MARK

CHARLES COOMBS

Philadelphia
THE WESTMINSTER PRESS

823
C 775

Library of Congress Catalog Card No.: 55-5759

PRINTED IN THE UNITED STATES OF AMERICA

37668

To my Nephew
John Olson
an avid reader
with a fine intelligence to prove it

1

I T WAS nearly nine o'clock when the three young people left the Oakmont City Public Library. The only relief in the crisp blackness of the night came from the reflection of the corner street light on the scattered patches of snow. Low clouds snuffed out any sign of moon or stars. The air had the feel of more snow coming.

Gordon Newhall, the tallest member of the trio, automatically turned the collar of his Windbreaker up around his neck, then stuffed his hands deep into his trouser pockets.

"Brr-rr," Julie Rogers said, pulling her brown shaggy-wool coat tighter around her. "I wonder where that spring thaw is hiding? The newspapers keep saying it's surely on its way. Can't arrive too soon for me."

"Be rugged, Sis," her older brother, Pete, said, thumping his chest Tarzan-fashion. "A little cold never hurt anybody."

"Cold has hurt a lot of people, Pete," Gordon spoke up. "It killed thousands of pioneers and Indians, and — well, during the big freeze of — "

"There you go," Pete cut in impatiently. "You always have to be so doggone logical."

"It wouldn't hurt you to be logical once in a while yourself, Pete," Julie scolded mildly. "It would be especially helpful during your Chemistry III mid-term tomorrow. You goof on that one and you'll be playing your baseball from the bleachers this year."

"Brr-rr, it sure *is* getting cold." Pete shuddered elaborately, as he fastened the two top buttons of his letterman's sweater. For a sophomore, Julie was amazingly adept at sprinkling salt on the sore spots. "Why do you have to bring up that frigid thought?"

"You shouldn't worry too much, Pete," Gordon encouraged. "That is, if any of the stuff sticks that we've been trying to drill into that cranium of yours all week."

"Cranium?"

"I suppose you'd call it a noggin."

"Then let's call it a noggin. Gordon, you always complicate everything."

"Pete, I don't see how you can talk like that to Gordon," Julie said. "Not after all he has done for you, trying to help you get ready for that mid-term."

"We neighbors have to stick together," Pete said. "Gordon knows if he doesn't help me I'm liable to huff and puff and blow his house down."

But Pete's gruffness was ninety-nine per cent bluff. He really appreciated the help the more studious boy had been giving him the past few evenings at the public library. He was even willing to admit somewhat grudgingly that Julie had been a help also. More than once she had calmed the rising storm in him, when he was seriously considering chucking the whole academic program and sending for an application to join the

8

Foreign Legion.

Yet, even during his darkest moments of faltering, Pete's thoughts had always drifted off to the baseball season which was fast approaching. Campus rumor had it that he was not only a cinch for first base, but was the leading candidate for team captaincy. And to Pete that was no small potatoes. He was a senior, with graduation only short months away. He had good enough grades in everything except his science courses. It was only natural that he was keeping a weather eye out for any loose college scholarship that might blow in his direction. Common sense would indicate that a good athletic standing just might fan the breeze a bit.

He remembered also that Gordon had been extremely helpful in keeping him eligible for nearly three years — at least, insofar as his science courses were concerned. And they were concerned plenty when it came to eligibility.

But Pete would have liked Gordon anyway. Nature had taken care of that. They were opposites, and wasn't there a standard saying that opposites attract opposites, or some such thing? Gordon was a tall, thin fellow, with sharp brown eyes which usually peered out through horn-rimmed glasses. Unlike Pete, Gordon was not much of an athlete. In fact he showed little interest in school sports, except in the role of side-line spectator. But Pete knew that what his scientific-minded friend lacked in physical prowess he more than made up for in mental gymnastics.

Although the two boys had practically nothing in common — except that they were both seventeen years old, and seniors at Oakmont High — they had lived

9

next door to each other for six years. Their friendship, like the giant oak from the little acorn, had simply grown.

Only on certain occasions was Pete's younger sister, Julie, allowed in on their plans. At the particular moment one thing in her favor was that she had a fair knowledge of basic science. She also had a full understanding of her brother's temperament. These two factors had established her value in the hectic evenings of cramming chemical knowledge into Pete's head, a head much more disposed to double plays than to hydrochloric acid. So, in his subtle manner, Gordon had included Julie in on the task of preparing Pete for the following day's Chemistry III exam.

Now the three of them walked down the main street of Oakmont City. They turned north at the far edge of the business district and headed out on Beaver Street. The night seemed to close in as the corner street lights became less frequent.

"Let's cut over to Westlake," Julie suggested after they had gone about three blocks. "I'd like to see if the school's open."

"At nine o'clock at night?" Pete scoffed. "Sis, you get the nuttiest notions."

"What's nutty about that?" Julie argued. "There might be a P.T.A. meeting going on, or something."

"I didn't notice an announcement of anything like that in the last issue of the school paper," Pete insisted. "Besides, what difference does it make whether the school's open or not? I get more than enough of it during the day."

"Well, I'd like to get in if I can," Julie explained.

10

"I forgot to take my English book home this afternoon. I need to review a couple chapters for my test tomorrow. The book's in my locker. It'd take only a jiffy to get it and —"

"Phooey. Of all the lame-brained —"

"What difference does it make, Pete?" Gordon spoke up. "It's not out of our way any to go past the school. Why make it sound like a big deal? Come on."

Pete swallowed any further protest. After all, with his usual logic, Gordon was right.

A few minutes later they approached the high school, which faced on Westlake Avenue. Oakmont High covered a full block. There were no automobiles parked in front. The campus appeared completely deserted. The main building, a massive brick structure honeycombed with offices, hallways, and classrooms, sat far back among the trees, about fifty yards from the street. The main building was flanked on each side by lesser classroom structures which had been added as Oakmont City had expanded its population.

From where the three young people now stood, they were unable to see the dome-roofed gymnasium, which was some distance behind the main building and next to the athletic field.

Except for one small section of second floor windows, the entire school was dark.

"Well," Pete said to Julie, "as you can plainly see, there is no P.T.A. meeting, no mothers-and-daughters banquet, no open house, no nothin' taking place. Of course, I told you so. But, then, I'm only your bigger and smarter brother."

"Lay off, Pete," Gordon warned. "I can't see how

11

we're any the worse off for coming this way. Say, I wonder what Professor Nordland would be doing up there at this time of night?"

"Professor Nordland?" Julie said, puzzled. "Up where, Gordon?"

"Those lights. That's the chemistry lab."

"Yeah. Guess you're right," Pete substantiated.

"Maybe the janitor is in there cleaning up," Julie suggested.

"Un-uh," Gordon grunted. "Professor Nordland won't let the janitor clean the lab unless he's right there to supervise it. Too many chemicals and acids and stuff. The janitor usually does it right after the final period."

"Well, if Prof Nordland's up there," Pete said, "I bet I know what he's doing."

"What's that, Pete?" Gordon said.

"He's trying to figure out some new and fiendish experiment to flunk me out on tomorrow."

Julie laughed. "I don't imagine he would have to do very much figuring," she said.

"You know Professor Nordland isn't that kind of man, Pete," Gordon said seriously.

"Just count on you to come to Nordland's rescue any time," Pete taunted. "What is there about him that brings out the good Samaritan in you, anyway?"

"He's just a real swell teacher," Gordon insisted.

"Sure, sure."

"After all, you haven't exactly gone out of your way to make him like you, Pete."

"Gordon's right," Julie seconded. "The way you smelled up the whole school with that mixture of hydrogen sulphide that day wasn't the best way to win a popularity contest with your chemistry teacher."

"A slight mix-up of formulas," Pete said, grinning over the memory of the noxious event that had filled the school with the odor of overripe eggs. " All an unfortunate accident, you know."

" I'll bet," Julie said.

"That other little business of going around the lab and slyly dusting a little gentian violet powder on the fellows' arms wasn't part of Professor Nordland's chemistry course, either," Gordon reminded.

Pete laughed. The light dusting of the powder hadn't been noticeable to any of the fellows at first. " But it sure was a riot when the guys started to wash up after class," Pete said, "and their arms turned that beautiful purple! Wow! " The memory still delighted him, although the extra work that Professor Nordland had doled out to him dimmed the achievement slightly.

Gordon had shown a certain amount of disgust with Pete on both occasions. Ever since the new head of the science department had arrived, Gordon had been his " man Friday."

Professor Nordland had transferred to Oakmont High nearly three years ago. He had formerly been a college professor some place out on the Coast. Campus rumor had it that the damp coastal climate hadn't agreed with him.

Without currying any special favors, Gordon had almost automatically become Professor Nordland's star science student. Everyone who knew him expected it to be so; for Gordon had been the " brain " in the science classes ever since his junior high days.

In due course of time Gordon seemed to think upon Professor Nordland in terms of halos. In his spare hours he usually could be found in the high school chemistry lab, either working on some experiment of his own or assisting Professor Nordland.

All this business, Pete figured, was O.K. with him since neither Gordon nor Professor Nordland was worth a hoot in the batter's box anyway. With Pete, if you couldn't make the grade as an athlete, you might just as well be a scientist— or anything.

Now, in the mellow glow from the corner street light, Pete noticed the thoughtful expression on Gordon's face. The boy kept his eyes on the lighted windows of the second floor. Things like a piece of blue litmus paper, a smear of swamp water under a microscope, or a single light burning in a school building usually set Gordon's mind to working in terms of causes and effects.

" I just thought of something," Pete said.

" What's that? " Julie asked suspiciously.

" Well, maybe it would be a good idea if we waited and walked home with Professor Nordland," Pete suggested. " Don't like to see a schoolteacher feeling lonesome." Actually it had occurred to Pete that there might be certain psychological advantages of such a fellowship with the professor on the eve of a midterm exam.

" It wouldn't do you a bit of good, Pete," Gordon said, looking into Pete's mind. " Professor Nordland doesn't go for that apple-polishing routine."

" Well, we might as well be on our way," Julie said. " It's quite apparent that the school is locked up. I'll just have to get here a little early in the morning and do some cramming."

They were just starting to turn away, when it happened. It happened with such an unexpected suddenness that even months later the three of them were unable to agree fully on what actually took place.

It began with a dazzling blaze of light which filled the upstairs windows of the chemistry lab. At the same moment that the ground around them was bathed with a yellowish brilliance, the muffled roar of the explosion smashed at their ears. The crisp tinkle of shattering glass filled out the mixture of frightening sound, as the laboratory windows blew outward.

Then there was a hollow silence, almost an aching silence.

The three Oakmont students stood rooted to the spot, immobilized by the suddenness and violence of the explosion. Pete stared at the windows. They were dark now, except for a faint orange glow that began to grow in intensity as he watched. His heart seemed to have stopped beating. A dull, throbbing hurt spread along the small of his back.

Then he heard Gordon's breath go out of him in a long exhaling hiss — sounding much like the time he had hit a curb and ripped the valve stem out of his bike tire.

The glow inside of the upstairs room continued to grow brighter. Then it began to flicker.

"Fire!" Julie was the first to find her voice. "The — the lab's on fire!"

Gordon shook himself, as though to clear away a fog. Pete sensed the obvious effort Gordon was having in

15

trying to gather his senses, trying to locate his voice.

"We — we've got to do something!" Julie cried.

"Pete!" Gordon grabbed the other boy's arm. Come on! Quick!"

CHAPTER

2

Togetber the two boys hurdled the low hedge along the walk. They plowed through the semi-slush of the straw-covered bulb garden. Then Pete heard Julie's lighter footsteps close behind. He didn't bother to call back in an effort to stop her, although he didn't feel this was a thing for a girl to get mixed up in. From long experience he knew that his younger sister would do just about what she wanted to, anyway.

Pete had never figured Gordon as being particularly fast on his feet. Yet there wasn't a half-second's difference in their time as they took the wide concrete steps to the main entrance of the school building in giant leaps. Julie was not far behind.

Gordon grabbed the brass handles of the heavy twin oak doors and heaved outward. The doors didn't budge. Pete reached past him and added his strength. Nothing happened.

"Fraid we can't make it," Gordon said breathlessly.

"Maybe the side door," Pete suggested quickly.

"No. They'll all be locked."

Julie stepped back, looked upward toward the orange glowing windows, and cupped her hands around her mouth. "Professor Nordland!" she called.

Silence.

Gordon moved quickly to the window of the principal's office, which was to the left of the main entrance. Pete followed, figuring that his friend intended to test the remote possibility of the window's being unlocked. But Gordon had something else in mind.

Before Pete realized what was happening, Gordon plunged his arctic through the window. A shower of glass fell around them, as Gordon quickly cleared away the jagged edges of the window with the heel of his rubber boot.

"This way, Pete," he said. "Hurry! Don't get cut. Watch your hands!" He swung his leg over the sill and leaped gingerly inside. Glass crunched beneath his feet. Pete followed carefully. Before either boy could stop her, Julie was standing beside them in the darkness of the principal's office.

"Gordon," Pete said, as the realization of what they had just done struck him, "we could get into a lot of trouble for this. Maybe — maybe what we saw up there was just part of some experiment that Professor Nordland's doing. Maybe he was splitting an atom or something. Look, pal, let's get out of here before — "

"It's a cinch you don't know much about explosions, Pete," Gordon said quickly. "You can be mighty sure that was no part of any experiment."

"Of course, he's right," Julie agreed. "No regular experiment is going to make a flash like that and — or blow out all the windows."

Pete had to admit that it was logical reasoning.

Gordon led the way cautiously out into the hallway. Except for a slight glow of illumination from the distant corner street light that filtered through the typing-room windows, the locker-lined hallway was dark as a roll of tar paper.

Julie's hand fumbled along the wall searching for a light switch, but she was unable to locate one.

" Pete," Gordon said, " follow me. Julie, maybe it would be better if you didn't try to come any farther."

" Don't worry about me," Julie said out of the dark-ness.

" Where to? " Pete asked.

" The lab." Gordon began to grope his way through the nearly pitch-blackness toward the stairs leading up to the second floor. Pete followed a few paces behind, barely able to keep his friend in sight.

As they reached the first landing, Gordon said, " Grab that fire extinguisher, Pete."

" What extinguisher? "

" There on the wall. Don't be dumb. You pass it ten times a day."

True, Pete realized vaguely, a little ashamed that he had had to ask. Although he could scarcely make it out, he felt along the wall, located the cylinder, and lifted it off its bracket.

Gordon's footsteps were already receding along the hallway overhead. Cradling the heavy extinguisher carefully in his arms, Pete followed.

Gordon was cautiously inching the lab door open by the time Pete caught up to him. The muffled crackle of flames filtered through the door and echoed down the hall. Pete took a firmer grip on the fire extinguisher.

" Stand back, Pete," Gordon warned. " There might be a flashback."

18

The ominous tone in the other boy's voice was sufficient to crowd Pete back against the far wall of the hallway. Gordon carefully jockeyed the door open, slowly, as if there were someone pushing against it from the other side.

"O.K., Pete," he cried, as the door went all the way open, and he flung up an arm to shield his face, "shoot it over in the corner there."

Pete stepped inside with the extinguisher. He fell back a moment as the hot blast hit his face. Then he eased forward again and pointed the small brass nozzle in the direction Gordon indicated. Nothing happened.

"Turn it over!" Gordon shouted.

It didn't make much sense, but Pete twisted the nozzle over.

"Not the nozzle; the cylinder, you sap!" Gordon's shout this time had definite overtones of urgent disgust.

Although Gordon was not given to dishing out pointed remarks, nor Pete to taking them, the occasion did not seem to warrant argument. Pete tipped the fire extinguisher over end for end. Results were instantaneous. The fire hadn't had time to catch a firm hold on paint or woodwork. Pete played the thin foamy stream along the section of wall and cabinets that was being licked by the blaze. As the fire receded against the onslaught of extinguisher fluid, the smoke thickened.

Both boys began to cough. A more delicate cough behind them indicated that Julie had not seen fit to stay downstairs. The last flickering flame was gone by the time the extinguisher spluttered empty. Pete set the copper cylinder on the floor and began to fumble along the wall for a light switch.

"Explosion would have knocked the light out, Pete," Gordon said simply. The huskier boy stopped groping.

The air began to clear, as the billowing smoke was sucked outside through the shattered laboratory windows. The room remained quite dark, with the hazy gray pall of smoke giving it an eerie effect.

"I'll try the office light," Gordon said. "Explosion probably didn't reach it."

Pete heard his friend crunching through the rubble on the floor, as he made his way to the small, almost closet-sized room off the lab. Once it had been a small storage room. In recent years it had served as Professor Nordland's private, if cramped, office.

The light flashed on. Enough glow filtered through the open doorway to reveal the scene of recent and sudden violence. A cyclone couldn't have left more devastation than was dimly apparent there in the upstairs chemistry room. Broken glass was everywhere. Remnants of test tubes, beakers, and flasks lay around in jagged disarray. Bits of glass tubing were scattered all over the room. One three-inch piece projected spearlike from the blackboard, testifying to the force of the explosion. Several Bunsen burners dangled over the sides of the cabinets from their short lengths of red rubber hose.

Most of the supply bottles that had been kept on shelves along the walls were now a brittle tangle on the floor. A pool of seething, varicolored fluid spread out across the oiled hardwood. The predominant smell was sulphur, which fumed up from a spilled carboy of sulphuric acid. The pungent odor started the young people into renewed spasms of coughing. Gordon felt his way along the far side of the room, where a few gallon jugs — some still unbroken — were lined up on the floor. He picked out a jug half full of fluid. Pete caught a quick glance at the label. In the semidarkness he could only make out sodium something-or-other. Wrenching off the cap, Gordon poured the contents over the simmering puddle on the floor. The fumes quickly subsided.

" That stuff neutralizes the acid," Gordon explained briefly.

With the room clearing, Julie slipped through the doorway and stood beside her two companions. There was a strange silence among them as they stood in the quiet aftermath of the excitement.

Later accusations were to censor them severely for not having called the police and fire departments at that time, if not earlier. Yet some of those who did the criticizing might well have been even more confused, had they been plunged suddenly into a similar situation. There is no groove in which the young mind works. Pete admitted later that, as he stared around him at the scene of recent explosive violence, his mind was going like a Fourth-of-July pinwheel. But none of the sparks were fanned into a single thought with any definite direction or purpose.

Gordon, the more organized and logical thinker under most circumstances, also seemed to be having a bit of trouble getting his train of thought on a through track. Pete watched him, wondering what came next.

He thought numbly of how he would know just what to do had the emergency occurred on the athletic field or inside of the gym. Those were his provinces. Each base line, yard stripe, hurdle, or basket presented challenges. Almost instinctively, through years of practice and a natural athletic ability, he would have known what to do.

But here in the chemistry laboratory, with the acrid fumes just clearing enough to make normal breathing possible, he was at a loss. He watched Gordon. Waited.

Gordon was intent on surveying the surrounding damage. Pete could almost hear the wheels whirring inside the sandy-thatched head, as Gordon's eyes played slowly over the dim scene.

The explosion seemed to have occurred in the corner of the room to the right of the doorway, for there the scene of the violence seemed at its worst. The charred doors of the sink cabinets were splintered as though they had been viciously pounded with a hammer. A metal stool lay twisted on the floor. A large heat-blistered gas cylinder, such as Pete had seen in factories or hospitals, was pushed halfway through the plastered wall.

Although the label had been blown and burned off, Pete knew what was in the cylinder — or what had been in it. Hydrogen. The chemistry class had been using it in recent experiments. In fact the hydrogen cylinder had been there all semester. It had been used as and when the various science classes needed a bit of hydrogen gas. The cylinder had been chained to the wall to prevent it from being tipped over or moved around.

The chain had been ripped away by the explosion. The gauge and shutoff-valve assembly at the top of the cylinder had been broken and twisted. It was obvious to Pete that the cylinder was now empty.

He noticed, then, that of the various Bunsen burners dangling over the edges of the sink cabinets by their short lengths of rubber hose, only one was burning. A small bluish gas flame flickered from its spout.

"Well, what do you make of it all, Gordon?" Julie asked finally.

"I'd say someone's been playing with fire," Pete put in casually. In all honesty he couldn't be too concerned over an accident to the chemistry lab. Too bad, of course, but one of those things.

"This is a lousy time for bum jokes, Pete," Gordon scolded. "There — there are sure lots of things that could stand explaining about this."

"Like what?"

"Well, in the first place, why was the light on up here? Why isn't Professor Nordland around? And how come that Bunsen burner's lighted?"

"Maybe during the explosion something hit against the pet cock and turned on the gas," Pete said. "The fire was plenty hot enough to light it."

"It sounds possible, Gordon," Julie backed up her brother.

"Sure. Possible." Gordon admitted. "But what would have set off the hydrogen in the first place, then? There had to be a fire to ignite it."

"You think the hydrogen caused the explosion?" Pete asked.

"What else? Everything seemed to begin right

around that corner where the cylinder is."

"But how?"

"Look, fellows," Julie interrupted, "in case it hasn't occurred to either of you, it seems to me that someone else should know about this. The police, or the fire department, or the principal, or —"

"Golly, guess we forgot," Pete said, recognizing the sense in his sister's observation. "But you'd think there'd be someone here by now. That explosion must have been loud enough to bring some neighbors tearing over."

"The closest homes are nearly two blocks away," Julie reminded.

It was true. The high school was located out on the west edge of town. Now that Pete thought of it, he could understand how the three of them were the only ones to know about the small-scale disaster.

"That's right," Gordon said, nodding agreement. "We've got to notify someone. But first let's look around a little." His gaze wandered off across the room, to the four other rows of sink cabinets which made up the Oakmont High chemistry lab. The farther away they were from the corner where the hydrogen cylinder was stored, the less pronounced was the damage. Yet, there was no place where the effect of the explosion had not been felt, where things were not charred and blistered and otherwise damaged.

"Look, pal," Pete said, "we've played hero long enough. Who'd ever thought that I'd end up lending a hand to keep a school from burning down? Particularly a chemistry lab. Enough's enough. And Julie's right. I'm going downstairs to the phone in Mr. Walker's office and notify someone."

"Yeah, you're right," Gordon said slowly, as he continued to wander around the lab, threading his way thoughtfully between the rows of waist-high sink cabinets. "Kind of forgot, I guess."

Pete started for the door. Julie stepped over to turn off the lone flickering Bunsen burner. They both froze as Gordon's strangled exclamation filled the room.

"Oh-h! Oh-h!" It was a painful sob that sent a chill coursing along Pete's spine. "Julie! Pete! Here!"

Pete spun around. Gordon was nowhere in sight in the dimly lighted room.

"Where'd he go?"

"Back toward those rear cabinets, I think," Julie said.

Pete crunched his way through the broken glass that littered the aisleway. He glanced between the rows of cabinets as he went. In the third aisleway, he spotted Gordon's shadowy figure. He was down between the cabinets, kneeling over a dark form. Pete moved closer in order to see through the dim light.

"Holy smoke!" he gasped, peering down over his friend's shoulder. "It — it's Prof Nordland!"

The chemistry teacher was lying face down, but his head was turned slightly sideways; so, even in the dim light, there was no mistaking his identity. He was wearing his familiar loose-fitting dark-blue wool sweater, with its mottling of chemical stains, that had become a regular trade-mark with the students. During winter classes, Professor Nordland usually substituted that sweater for his suit coat, thus preserving his suit from acids and bleaches. A rubber apron, which now lay crumpled beneath him, protected his trousers.

Pete could barely make out his face. The teacher's eyes were partially open. Even in the scant light his skin seemed chalky.

" He — he must be hurt bad," Pete said. " I'll tear after some help. We'd better get him to a hospital quick."

Julie had stopped at one end of the sink cabinet. Her lower lip quivered until she bit down on it. She leaned against the cabinet to steady herself.

Gordon straightened up slowly. He looked at Julie, then at Pete. Pete could barely see the taller boy's mouth move. Yet no sound emerged. He saw the wet streaks glisten along each side of Gordon's straight nose.

" Pete, I — I — think — he's dead! "

Pete's stomach flipped over and he leaned heavily against the cabinet. Something thumped wildly inside of his chest.

" Julie," Gordon said, " maybe you better go downstairs."

Pete tried a few times and was finally able to manage a swallow. His mind spun in confusion. The one thought that rose above all others was the intense desire to get out of the lab. " I'll — I'll call the city hospital," he stammered, for lack of knowing what else to propose in such a situation.

" I think it might be better to call the police, Pete," Gordon suggested.

" Doesn't matter to me," Pete said. " Only I don't see exactly what the police have to do with — with — "

" Pete," Gordon interrupted. His voice had turned

26

strangely husky as he made a visible effort to control himself, "the police have everything to do with — with murder!"

Julie turned away with a sob, and walked unsteadily toward the door.

"Look, Gordon," Pete said, attempting to keep his own voice calm, and also striving to keep his eyes away from the crumpled body on the dimly lighted laboratory floor. "Look, fellow, don't — don't let this thing get you. It's bad enough if it's an accident. Accidents have happened before in chemistry labs. Else why do our textbooks have so many warnings about not doing this and being careful about doing that?"

"So what are you driving at, Pete?" the other boy said thoughtfully, not seeming to pay particular heed to his companion's words.

"Just this, pal," Pete said. "Don't try to make a mystery out of it. If Professor Nordland's dead, that's bad enough."

"There — there's no doubt about his being dead, Pete," Gordon said.

"Well, don't start making a murder out of it. This sure isn't any time to be playing games, and — Say, just what makes you think it wasn't an accident in the first place?"

"Fellows," Julie said weakly from the doorway, "let's get away from here."

"Just a minute, Sis," Pete said, still eying the taller

27

boy suspiciously. "Maybe Gordon knows something about this that we don't. All right, pal, give. Just what gives you the idea it wasn't all an accident?"

Gordon removed his glasses and wiped away the fog that had condensed on them from his sweaty forehead. His hands shook as he slipped the glasses back on.

"Pete," he said, "don't ask questions. Not now. I could be wrong."

"About its being murder, you mean?"

"Yeah."

"Sure you're wrong. You're dead wrong." Pete hadn't meant the pun, and he didn't miss Gordon's sharp glance.

"Have it your way," the studious boy said. "There are things you don't know. Things that a lot of people don't know."

"Such as?"

"Not now, Pete," Gordon said impatiently. "I repeat, someone had better go down to Mr. Walker's office and phone the police."

"Yeah, you're right," Pete admitted, noting the urgency in Gordon's voice. Besides, right at the moment nothing suited him quite as well as getting away from the chemistry laboratory with its fresh signs of tragedy. "Julie, you want to come?" But his sister didn't seem to hear, so he started off alone.

The hallway was still dark. As he felt his way slowly down the stairs, Pete scolded himself inwardly for not knowing where the light switches were located. He supposed there was a master switch panel someplace. Out of the way, probably, so that the students wouldn't make a game of flicking the lights on and off. A slight

28

glow in the lower hallway enabled him to move a little faster toward Mr. Walker's office. Once again he was unable to locate a light switch. He groped his way inside, crunching through the glass from the broken window. He felt along the principal's desk until his hand came in contact with the telephone.

His finger sought the last hole on the dial. He spun for Operator, waited several rings, then heard the feminine voice on the other end. " Number, please."

" Police," Pete said quickly. " Get me the police department . . . please."

There was no hesitation on the operator's part as she relayed the call.

" Oakmont Police. Sergeant Haskins speaking," a husky voice said.

The words began to tumble out of Pete's mouth in a confused torrent. " Oakmont High . . . explosion . . . chemistry lab . . . fire . . . Professor Nordland . . . dead . . . hurry . . ."

" Hold on. Who's talking? What kind of joke — "

But Pete had stopped listening. Even as the police sergeant was talking, Pete saw a shadow — about man-size — glide past the doorway of the principal's office. Sergeant Haskins' voice trailed off, as Pete silently lowered the phone back to its cradle.

Pete stood, not daring to move, and trying to unscramble his thoughts. This whole thing was ridiculous — discovering a corpse, listening to Gordon speak of murder, seeing shadows. It was grim fantasy, something straight out of a nightmare. Pete figured that he had gone along just about as far as he cared to in the whole frightening travesty. This was a time to let himself quietly out through the broken window of Mr. Walker's office, and add a good deal of distance between himself and whatever grim folly was taking place there in the Oakmont High School building. This sort of thing just didn't happen in real life.

Yet evidently it did, and he couldn't simply walk away from it and leave his own sister in danger. Nor could he leave Gordon stranded, as far as that went. Difficult as it was to convince himself that the happenings of the past fifteen minutes were actual and not imaginative, the necessity for some kind of action seemed very real.

No, it was no dream, no fictional figment of someone's imagination. Pete knew it, as well as he knew that the shadow that had just flitted past the doorway was of solid human origin.

Choices of action quickly slendered down to one. He had to investigate that shadow. He didn't believe in ghosts. He also felt as capable of handling himself as the next guy. Whoever owned that shadow was made of bone and muscle, the same as he. Slowly the spirit of combat which ran deep in Pete's blood replaced whatever fear he had felt. Physical action was his meat.

He eased out through the open doorway, trying his best to avoid stepping on the pieces of broken window that littered the floor, but was only partially successful. The brittle crunching underfoot seemed loud in his ears — certainly loud enough to give away his position to anyone prowling the hallways.

Once in the long locker-lined corridor, he moved silently on tiptoe. He craned his neck around the corner, then drew it back quickly. In the dim glow that filtered into the hallway from the outside street lamp, he had caught a slight movement of a dark form against a slightly lighter background of the gray book lockers. The movement was just beyond the study-hall doorway. A small movement, but unmistakable. Pete could even make out the general size of the figure. A little taller, perhaps, than himself, but, from the quick and inconclusive glance, no huskier.

Pete felt the muscles along his shoulder blades and across his chest begin to tighten. It was the same feeling that he often experienced at the beginning of a crucial football game, or when the basketball team took to the hardwood floor. It was the feeling of strength flowing into him. The coach called it " manufacturing adrenaline "; the players called it " pregame butterflies." Whatever it was, Pete had it now. Had it strong. And, in an emergency, a fellow like Pete was often more apt to depend upon his strength and agility of muscle than upon his mental prowess. Three years of varsity sports had prepared him for more than just blocking, open-field running, aiming for the basket, or relaying a double-play ball.

He was far better attuned to physical emergencies than to mental ones.

He started down the hallway — slowly, silently, gaining momentum with each step. Six feet from the shadow, he launched himself through the air. It was as solid a tackle as he ever had made. After the hard contact, he kept driving forward, although his feet slipped miserably on the oiled hardwood floor.

With a startled grunt, his adversary gave way. They

31

fell heavily and went skidding down the floor together.

Pete heard something hard and metallic clattering along ahead of them. Suddenly the two tangled bodies came to a painful stop up against a drinking fountain.

Pete loosened his grip around the person's legs and was getting ready to start finishing the thing off with his fists when a hurt voice spoke up.

" You — you sap! "

" Gordon! "

" Of course, nitwit. Who were you expecting, Snow White? Get off me, you moose."

The two boys untangled themselves slowly. Pete was torn between offering Gordon an apology and socking him on the nose. Under less tense circumstances his gangly friend would never have gotten away with calling him a sap, a nitwit, and a moose — all within a matter of seconds. Tonight, though, Pete seemed able to overlook many things.

" Where's Julie? " he demanded quickly.

" She's upstairs."

" In the lab? With that — that — "

" She's at the top of the stairs," Gordon assured. " She waited up there while I came down here."

" While you came down here for what? " Pete demanded.

" Hey, what's going on down there? " Julie's voice called through the darkness from the far end of the hallway, and above. " Sounded like a — a train wreck or something."

" Everything's O.K., Julie," Gordon assured her. " We'll be back up there in a minute. Pete, were you able to get the police? "

" I think so," Pete said. " But about that time you went sneaking past the door, and I quit talking. Think I got the message out all right, though. Hey, what're you doing down there on the floor? "

Pete realized that Gordon's voice had been coming from floor level. In the faint light he saw that his friend had dropped to his knees and was groping around as though searching for something.

" I — I'm trying to find the box I was carrying when you decided to play hero," the other boy said.

" What kind of box? " Pete asked. Then he recalled having heard the metallic clank of something skidding across the floor right after he had tackled Gordon.

" Just a plain tin box," his friend said. " You know — the kind that — oh, oh, here it is! "

Gordon's sigh of relief was unusually elaborate for his quiet nature. Getting back to his feet, he went to the lockers. Pete saw him half feeling, half squinting his way along the row. Then he came to a stop. Pete heard the clicks of a combination lock as Gordon spun the dial. In the dim glow Pete could see the box that his friend held. It was fairly small: less than a foot long, about six or eight inches wide, and three or four inches high. Pete couldn't make out the color exactly, but it looked very much like one of those inexpensive dark green " strong boxes " which people purchase at hardware stores for the safekeeping of receipts, insurance papers, and things.

" What the dickens is that for? " Pete asked.

Without answering, Gordon put the box in his locker and slammed the door. He was just spinning the combination lock when the whine of approaching sirens

33

filtered through the broken window of the principal's office.

"Well, I guess Sergeant Haskins decided my call was no joke, after all," Pete said happily. " Man, I'll be glad to see some friendly faces around here! "

"Pete, Gordon," Julie called. " The police are coming! "

"We know," Pete called back. " Better stay there, Julie. We'll be with you in a jiffy."

Pete felt Gordon's hand on his arm. "Hey, let go. What's the — "

"Look, Pete," the other boy said in a low but hurried voice, " whatever you do, don't make any mention of that box to the police. No matter what. Promise? "

"You crazy, guy? " Pete scoffed. " What's so secret about a cheap tin box, and — "

"It's very important; and very secret, Pete," Gordon said emphatically. " Promise? "

"But why? " Pete tried to think of some possible reason why Gordon should be so secretive about the tin box. " You want to get us in trouble with the police or something? "

"It won't get us in trouble with the police," Gordon assured. " And I tell you it's important that no one knows about that box. You've got to trust me."

"But I don't get it," Pete argued. " Why so mysterious? Give me one reason why — Say, where did that box come from, anyway? "

"Pete, there's no time for explanations," Gordon said. " I'll tell you later. But promise you won't mention it to anybody. Promise? "

Pete had never seen his friend so insistent.

34

" O.K., pal, I promise. I don't know why, but I'll go along with you — for a while, anyway."

" Thanks, Pete," the other boy said. " And don't worry, everything will be all right."

" Hey, the police are pulling up out front."

" Better see if we can find some light switches," Gordon suggested. " I think there's a block of them at the far end of this row of lockers. See if you can find them. I'll open the front door."

Pete fumbled around until he found the switch box right where Gordon had mentioned it would be. In fact, it dawned on Pete guiltily that he had passed those switches several times daily for nearly three years without once bothering to mark the fact in his mind.

Now he flicked the toggle switches. As the lights began to blaze along the hallway, a small group of people surged in through the front door, which Gordon had opened. The group consisted of Lieutenant Coleman, Oakmont City's chief of detectives, a couple of patrolmen whom Pete didn't recognize, and Lloyd Dyer, star reporter for the Oakmont City *Globe*.

Everyone began talking at once. Then, out of the confusion of sound, Pete heard Julie's strangely high-pitched voice.

" Pete! Pete! Look! "

Glancing toward her on the stair landing, Pete saw that she was pointing toward the stairs nearest him which led down to the basement area. He turned quickly and glanced into the lower darkness where the main floor lights didn't quite reach.

In the shadows he saw a man's face peering upward. It was too dark, and he was at too great a distance, for

Pete to make out who it was. But for a moment their eyes met.

Then the face ducked away quickly, leaving only darkness at the bottom of the stairs.

Bewildered, Pete was still staring toward the darkness of the basement when Julie scurried down the stairs and rushed to his side. " Pete, did — did you see it? " she asked anxiously.

" See what? " he said absently.

" The face, of course."

" So you saw it too."

" Why do you think I yelled at you? " Julie said sharply. " Now, quit being dopey, and wake up. Who do you think it was? "

" Maybe it wasn't anybody," Pete said. " Maybe our imaginations are getting the best of us. Most I could see was eyes. Could have been a cat even. There are some around the school, you know. And the janitor leaves them inside overnight sometimes. Keeps the mouse population down."

" It couldn't have been a cat." Julie stared at him in disbelief. " That's ridiculous, and you know it. What's the matter with you, Pete? "

" Matter with me? " Pete said. " You tell me something. Who got a better look at it, you or me? "

" Well, you were closer, all right, but — "

" I'm not saying it *was* a cat, and I'm not sure it was

36

a person," Pete said. " Not absolutely, positively. Golly, Sis, things have been happening so fast that — well, I wouldn't be surprised if a camel caravan suddenly started marching out of the typing room or something."

" Maybe we should tell the police anyway," Julie suggested.

" And get the horse laugh if they find some cat prowling around downstairs? If I'm having hallucinations, I want to keep them to myself. Come on. Let's go see what's up."

The two young people hurried to join the group that was gathering at the angle of the hallway near Mr. Walker's office. Gordon was just getting well into his story of the evening's happenings. Lieutenant Coleman listened attentively without interruption, as the tall boy related the straight facts of the past fifteen or so minutes. Pete thought, though, that the detective kept a pretty steady eye on Gordon — possibly even a suspicious eye.

Pete didn't know how many of his theories Gordon had mentioned to Lieutenant Coleman before he and Julie joined the group. But he hoped his science-minded friend had been able to restrain himself. Gordon was occasionally prone to get wild ideas. And, for Pete's money, this was a good time to leave wild ideas unspoken.

Nor did Pete miss the fact that Gordon made absolutely no mention of the tin box which was now hidden in his book locker. But silence on that subject was expected, since Gordon had gone to the extreme in swearing Pete to secrecy.

The quick conference in the main floor hallway

broke up, and the group started on upstairs. Lloyd Dyer fell in beside Pete.

" Hi, pal," he said. " What kind of monkey business is going on here tonight? I picked up the call on my radio, and high-tailed it over here. Almost beat the police." He grinned. " What cooks? "

" You couldn't prove anything by me, Mr. Dyer," Pete said. He was well acquainted with the *Globe* reporter. In fact, Pete considered the middle-aged newsman as a rather good friend. Along with his regular news gathering, Dyer did a considerable amount of school coverage. He was a welcome figure around the Oakmont campus, and a rabid sports fan. He had given Pete plenty of swell breaks in his sports news stories during the half year he had been on the staff of the *Globe*. Although much of the school's news was handed in by student correspondents, Dyer seemed to have the knack for sensing the bigger stories and being on hand to cover them himself. In the six months he had been on the *Globe* staff, Dyer had become as familiar a part of Oakmont High as the flagpole in the quad.

" Is it as bad as your friend makes it sound, Pete? " Dyer said now. He lifted his felt hat and raked long fingers through his thinning brown hair.

" It sure isn't good, Mr. Dyer," Pete answered. " You should have seen that explosion."

" What time did all this start? " the newsman asked. " Who found Professor Nordland's body, and — "

" I'll ask the questions, if you don't mind, Dyer," Lieutenant Coleman spoke back over his shoulder.

The reporter slipped Pete a wink. " The lieutenant

hasn't had a murder to play around with for a long time," he whispered. " Mustn't let anything crab his act."

As they approached the upstairs chemistry lab, the conversation died out. Lieutenant Coleman stopped in the doorway and took a long, all-encompassing glance into the dimly lighted room.

" Sergeant," he said to one of his men, " steal a light bulb from some other classroom." Then he turned to Gordon. " Newhall, where's the body? "

" It — he's back between the third row and the last row of cabinets," Gordon said.

" O.K., you come with me," the detective said. " The rest of you wait out here."

Pete watched Gordon, and saw the almost frightened concern on his friend's face. He wondered if Gordon was worried about the questions Lieutenant Coleman was certain to start shooting at him once they were alone in the lab. He wondered also if Gordon wasn't already beginning to regret having hidden the mysterious metal box. There was no doubt that the detective chief would take a dim view of such shenanigans, were they found out. And surely, Pete thought, the time would come when the box would have to be made known to the police. He just couldn't imagine what could have been on Gordon's mind to want to hide that box.

Pete and Julie walked over and sat on the top stair to wait. Lloyd Dyer joined them. He leaned back against the wall and fished in his pocket for a cigarette.

" No smoking in the high school, Dyer," a patrolman cautioned.

"Sorry, I forgot." The newsman dropped the pack back into his pocket.

The sergeant returned in a few minutes with a light bulb, and went on inside the lab room. Shortly a blaze of light seeped from beneath the door. The sergeant came back out.

"Give me the low-down, Pete," Lloyd Dyer said. "Just how did you kids happen to be around here when the explosion happened? And — "

"Mr. Dyer," the sergeant cut in, "you better wait and get your story from the lieutenant. He's not going to like it a bit if you start pumping these kids. Now, I'd advise you to sit tight. You know that the lieutenant always gives you newspapermen a fair shake."

Lloyd Dyer shrugged, but didn't pursue his questioning. They listened to the steady murmur of voices from inside. Pete wondered how well Gordon would stand up under the grilling of Lieutenant Coleman — if, indeed, that was what was taking place behind the lab door. Only once did Pete hear the police officer raise his voice. He wondered if the subject of the metal box had come up. Yet no one could know about it unless Gordon wanted it known. And he certainly had taken great pains thus far in preventing its being known.

After about ten minutes the laboratory door opened. Lieutenant Coleman poked his head out. His face was extremely grave. "All right," he said to Lloyd Dyer, "you can come in now. But don't touch anything. Nothing."

"What does it all figure, Lieutenant?" the newspaperman asked.

40

"It doesn't figure anything yet," the detective said. "But I don't want any messing around until we know more of what took place up here. The Newhall boy has a theory. Makes a bit of sense too. The physical aspects certainly indicate a possibility of murder. But, so far, one important item is missing."

"What's that?"

"A motive. What possible reason could anyone have for wanting to do away with a high school chemistry teacher?"

"Maybe he discovered how to make gold out of peach pits or something," Lloyd Dyer said.

"Let's save the jokes for the funny papers," the lieutenant scolded.

"Sorry," Dyer apologized. "Wasn't very clever, was it? Besides, I agree with you, a motive is a pretty important thing."

"One will turn up," the detective said positively, "providing it wasn't an accident."

"You have a point there too, Lieutenant," Lloyd Dyer said. "Just what makes you think it wasn't an accident?"

"Well, we don't need to go into that at the moment," the detective said. "Besides, that's police business. If you want to come in and look around, O.K. Just be careful. You'll have to report the news pretty much as you see it. I can't give you many details. As a matter of fact, I don't know many — yet."

Pete and Julie stayed in the hallway. "You want to go back in?" Pete asked.

"Heavens no," his sister said. "I hope I never have to see anything like that again in my whole life. Pete," she lowered her voice to a whisper, " what did Gordon do with that box? "

" You saw it? " Pete said, surprised.

" Of course. He tried to hide it from me, but I saw it when he brought it out of the lab, and started down the stairs. Why would he want to hide it from me? "

" I don't know," Pete said. " Wish I did."

" Anyway, he told me not to mention it to anyone," Julie said. " Made me promise."

" Then why are you telling me? " Pete asked accusingly.

" You knew it," Julie said. " Goodness, don't you think I heard you two chattering downstairs? What do you think is in it, Pete? "

" Haven't the slightest idea. Why? "

" I — I'm not at all sure that Gordon's doing the right thing by hiding it," Julie said. " Besides, I'm not so sure that I'm not a little suspicious of him."

" Gordon? " Pete said, staring at his sister. " Suspicious of Gordon? That's the craziest thing you've said in a long — " But Pete's words faded out. Why try to run a bluff with his own sister? After all, he was suspicious of Gordon too. Not suspicious that his friend would have anything to do with murder — if that was what it proved to be. But suspicious that Gordon was hiding valuable evidence in that box. Suspicious that Gordon knew a lot more about the whole affair than he was letting on.

" Sergeant," Lieutenant Coleman stepped to the doorway again, " another squad car just pulled up outside. Better have the men take a close look around the building. Check for unlocked windows or doors.

Watch out for footprints, or anything else that might have some bearing on this business."

The sergeant turned to leave.

" And," the chief detective added, " you'd better call the coroner."

Julie took hold of Pete's arm. Even before she spoke, Pete knew what was on her mind. " I don't think Gordon has any right to expect us not to mention that box. We could get into trouble."

" Yeah, you're right," Pete said, rising. " Maybe he's suffering from shock or something. Doesn't mean that we've lost our heads too."

" That's right," Julie said. " And we might be saving Gordon an awful lot of trouble."

" Yeah," Pete agreed, then turned toward the chemistry lab. " Oh, Lieutenant Coleman."

The detective turned in the doorway. " Not now, son," he said curtly. " Whatever you've got to say will hold a few minutes. Right now I've got plenty on my mind, and —"

" But, Lieutenant Coleman," Pete insisted, " this is important, and —"

Just then Pete saw Gordon's head poke up from behind the detective's shoulder. His friend stared at him. The expression in Gordon's eyes was a mixture of warning and imploring. Nor was there any indication in the expression that Gordon was not completely in control of his wits.

Also there was something in Gordon's look that reminded Pete once again of the fact that he had made a promise — a promise to make no mention of the metal box. Nothing in Gordon's expression gave any indica-

43

tion that he was relieving Pete of the responsibility of keeping his word.

"All right, what is it, son?" Lieutenant Coleman said impatiently.

It was almost too late to back out now. Pete glanced quickly at Julie. She too seemed to have seen Gordon's face behind the detective's shoulder. She lowered her eyes, as though suddenly ashamed that she and Pete had nearly abandoned their friend in a critical moment.

"No-nothing," Pete said. "Guess I was just thinking out loud."

He saw a smile flicker quickly on Gordon's face. But he didn't return it.

He was much too worried.

CHAPTER

5

Pete and Julie waited in the hallway while Lloyd Dyer went inside to fill in on the facts for his news story. Julie looked at the wall clock at the far end of the corridor. "It's nearly ten," she said. "Mother and Dad are going to start wondering where we are."

"Guess we should call home, at that," Pete said. But before the idea jelled into action, Lieutenant Coleman, Lloyd Dyer, and Gordon came back out of the chemistry lab.

"Well, that's about it for now," the detective said. "You kids might as well go on home. The sergeant can take you in the squad car. I'd better wait around here for the coroner."

44

Gordon said: " Come on, Julie, Pete. What d'ya say we go? "

Pete thought Gordon looked tired — sad and tired.

" Oh, by the way," Lieutenant Coleman spoke up as they were turning to leave. " I'll want all three of you at the police station by ten o'clock tomorrow morning. Few things I want to get straightened out."

" But," Pete started to protest, " I have a chemistry mid-term tomorrow just before ten, and — " Then he realized how ridiculous it must have sounded. Obviously, without Professor Nordland, there would be no Chemistry III mid-term as scheduled.

Strangely, the unexpected reprieve didn't make him the least bit elated.

" Come on, Pete," Gordon said again. " Our folks are probably beginning to wonder what's happened to us."

" Speaking of your folks," Lieutenant Coleman put in, " I'll have to ask you kids not to say any more than you have to about this. I'm not proposing that you attempt to deceive your parents. But if you do tell them, ask them to keep it confidential. If it isn't too awkward, I'd rather you didn't tell anyone until morning."

" Yes, sir, we understand," Pete said.

" People will know the whole story as soon as we crack it open," the detective said. " That's soon enough. Dyer, you be careful too. Stick to the facts, sparse as they are. Let the police do the theorizing."

" Whatever you say, Lieutenant," Lloyd Dyer said casually. " You never need to worry about the *Globe's* co-operation."

45

The three young people went downstairs together. The police sergeant followed. Pete noticed that Gordon was fidgety, somewhat hesitant in his movements. He kept glancing over his shoulder at the policeman.

"Sergeant," Gordon said as they reached the foot of the stairs, "there's really no need for you to drive us home. It's just a couple of blocks or so. We can manage easily."

Pete looked at his friend, puzzled. What possible reason could Gordon have for turning down a ride in a squad car? After all, it would be something to talk about later. How many of their school friends ever had a chance to ride in a police car?

"It's no trouble," the sergeant said.

"Well, we'd rather walk, anyway," Gordon insisted. "Besides, if we drive up to our houses in a police car, the neighbors are going to get mighty curious and start asking questions. And you know what Lieutenant Coleman said about keeping this thing quiet for a while."

Although Pete still would have liked to ride home in the squad car, there was something in Gordon's manner that prompted him to hold his tongue. Julie seemed to sense it also, and said nothing.

"Guess you make some sense, at that," the policeman acknowledged. "All right, have it your way. But head straight home. Don't worry about getting hauled in for curfew violation, though. This happens to be my territory." The sergeant turned and went back upstairs.

"What's the big idea of doing a crazy thing like that?" Pete demanded as soon as the policeman was out of sight. "I've got nothing against riding home in a squad car, long as I'm a guest of the city."

46

"It would have been fun, at that," Julie said.

"Yeah, it would have been," Gordon agreed.

"Then why did you call it off?"

They had reached the front door when Gordon stopped. He glanced around as though to make certain that the hallway was vacant. "We can't very well just leave that box in my locker," he said.

"I can," Pete said. "I think it was a silly idea to put it there in the first place. What if they call for a locker inspection tomorrow, or something?"

"That's exactly what I'm thinking about," the taller boy said.

"Gordon," Julie spoke up, "you must have a reason for it, but — but just why did you take that box out of the chemistry lab? Why did you hide it? What's in it?"

"Not now, Julie," Gordon said. "I can't tell you now. But we've got to get that box away from here."

"Where do you get that 'we' stuff?" Pete challenged. "If it's too big a secret to let Julie and me in on, then you do the worrying about it yourself. Come on, Julie."

Gordon grabbed Pete's arm. Pete whirled angrily, ready to knock the hand away. He changed his mind when he saw the worried expression on Gordon's face. "Look, pal," he said, "I don't like trouble any better than the next guy, especially with the police. Why don't you just get smart and turn that box over to Lieutenant Coleman? This playing cops and robbers isn't going to get us anyplace — unless it's in jail."

"I wish I could just turn it over to the police, Pete," Gordon said. "But I made a promise to Professor Nordland. I can't break it."

47

"What kind of promse?" Julie asked.

"I wish I could tell you, but I can't — not just yet. Believe me, though, it's really important that no one gets hold of that box. I'll tell you the whole thing as soon as I get a chance." He poked his head around the corner where a spur of the hallway angled past the principal's office. "We've got to sneak that box out of here. This may be our only chance."

"Sure, sure," Pete said. "And what happens if somebody sees us?"

"Everyone's upstairs," Gordon said.

Pete heard the low hum of voices from the general direction of the upstairs chemistry laboratory. "Doesn't mean everyone's going to stay up there," he said.

"Look," Gordon said flatly, "will you help me or won't you?"

Looking at him, Pete knew there was little choice. He wasn't the kind of guy who could abandon his friend at such a time. It was also obvious to Pete that whatever Gordon had in mind was of extreme importance. The scientific-minded boy was much too level-headed to be playing games at a time like this.

"What do you want us to do, Gordon?" Julie spoke up while Pete was still making up his mind.

"Julie, you stay here by the front door," Gordon instructed quickly. "Pete, you go down by the foot of the stairs below the chemistry lab. If either one of you hears anyone coming, give a cough."

"What are you going to be doing all this time?" Pete asked.

"I'm going to get the box out of my locker. And we've got to get it out of this building without being

48

seen," Gordon cautioned.

"But what if you just happen to bump into the coroner coming in, or some other policeman shows up?" Julie asked. "Fact is, there's another police car out there now. The one Lieutenant Coleman mentioned. Too dark to tell for sure, but there might even be someone sitting in it."

The boys followed her gaze through the open front door and out to the white-sided car.

"We'd better go out the side door," Gordon said.

"Maybe it's locked."

"They all open from the inside," Gordon said. "Just push against the bar."

Pete knew it was true. The bar on the inside of all exterior school doors was a safety factor. Regardless of the emergency, any pressure on the bar would open the door outward. Gordon seemed to have everything figured out, all right.

"Let's go," Gordon prompted. "No telling how long this floor will be vacant."

He tiptoed silently down the well-lighted hallway toward his locker. Pete and Julie moved swiftly but quietly to their designated posts. From his position at the foot of the stairs, Pete watched Gordon spin the combination to his lock. Even though the lights were on bright, the long locker-lined hallway, vacant except for Gordon, gave Pete an eerie feeling.

The steady murmur of voices continued to come from overhead. Pete couldn't see Julie, who was out of sight near the front door.

Then Pete heard the faint click as Gordon lifted the latch of his locker. He saw him reach inside and bring

49

out the dark-green metal box. Gordon glanced around quickly to see that everything was clear; then carefully closed his locker and spun the combination.

As Pete thought of it later, spinning the combination of the lock was almost like setting off the fuse of a carefully machined time bomb. In the next minute or so things couldn't have gone worse for the three young people, even if they had all been born under the wrong signs of the zodiac, had walked under too many ladders, or had all been served double whammy by a tribe of left-footed Zulus. Like grapes, their troubles came in clusters.

No sooner had Gordon closed his locker, and started up the hallway carrying the box, than Julie's artificial, but meaningful, warning cough echoed down the corridor.

" Pss-sst, Gordon," Pete called softly, " let's get out of here! "

The boy with the tin box needed no prompting. He started trotting toward Pete, who quickly left his post to meet him. They arrived at the center of the hall just as Julie hurried around the corner from where she had been standing guard near the main entrance. For a moment all three of them stood where they could get a good view of the open doorway and the broad concrete steps that led down to the front walk.

It was during that moment of indecision on just which may to move next that they were attracted by the commotion moving up the dark front steps and into the light that filtered outside from the hallway. Two uniformed policemen approached the open doorway. They were half leading, half pushing, a protesting

50

gray-haired man before them.

Gordon seemed temporarily at a loss what to do. He ducked the metal box behind him and backed up to the wall. " Hans Oberheath! " he gasped. " What's Hans Oberheath doing around here at this time of night? "

Several thoughts crowded through Pete's mind. Hans Oberheath was a part-time janitor around school. One quick look at Hans's frightened face, especially the eyes, and Pete knew it had been Hans who had peered upward from the basement area a little earlier that evening. Pete looked quickly at Julie. She nodded understandingly.

" I knew it wasn't any cat," she said.

And now Hans was holding back, protesting to the two policemen as best he could, considering that the elderly Dutchman was about the least communicative person Pete had ever known.

But there was another thought pushing into Pete's mind right at the moment. What if the policemen spotted the box? If its secret was as important as Gordon let on, this was no time to be losing possession of it. Despite his efforts, Gordon was having a difficult time hiding it behind his back. Pete had no doubt that, once inside the building and under the bright lights, the policemen surely would notice the metal box.

Pete saw that Gordon was trembling. His friend seemed to have drawn a blank in his thoughts, which certainly was not typical of him. Once again Pete's athletic training for applying action in moments of emergency came to the fore.

" Gordon," he whispered, " slip me the box. Go help those policemen. At least, act like you want to help.

51

Keep their attention away from me — just for a few seconds. I'll head out the side door. See what I mean?"

The logic of the suggestion was obvious. Without a word, Gordon slipped the box to Pete, at the same time turning his back toward the doorway so his body would help shield the action from the eyes of the approaching trio.

Quickly and quietly Pete turned, dodged around the corner into the main hallway, and headed for the side door. Julie rushed along beside him.

"Hurry, Pete," she prompted.

Pete needed no such urging. He moved as fast as he could without being overly noisy. He felt confident that the policemen coming up the front steps hadn't seen him. He could still hear the commotion, and assumed that Gordon was managing to delay them somehow, giving Pete and Julie a chance to get out of the building. Everything was working out all right, and Pete was mentally complimenting himself for some fast thinking and some speedy action when it was most needed.

He and Julie weren't ten feet from the side door when, from the corner of his eye, he saw a light blur of movement on the stairway. Glancing up, he saw Lloyd Dyer just starting down the stairs.

"Oh, Pete," Lloyd called as soon as he spotted the two young people, "you don't happen to know what happened when —"

But neither Pete nor Julie was in any mood to pause for a quiz. They hurried forward to the door.

"Hey, you kids," Dyer called after them. "What's the big hurry?" Then the newspaperman laughed.

" Say, what are you trying to hide — some kind of concealed weapon or something? "

Pete experienced a split second of complete indecision. Now that Lloyd Dyer had seen the box, wouldn't the intelligent thing be to call the whole thing off and surrender the mysterious parcel to Lieutenant Coleman? It seemed that Gordon had involved both him and Julie in a dangerous kind of game. Sometimes the sensible part of valor was to admit defeat, particularly when the odds were so overwhelmingly against you that to continue bucking them was sheer folly. And right at the moment, with Lloyd Dyer looking down on him and Julie — and taking full notice of the dark-green metal box — Pete felt as though the game surely was over. He was backed up to his goal line, ten seconds left to play, and the other team out ahead by two touchdowns.

Then Julie spoke at his elbow. " Keep going, Pete," she prompted. " We — we can't let Gordon down now."

" Hey, hold up a second, Pete," Dyer called.

Although Pete had slowed down while his mind paused to deliberate the situation, both Julie's words and Lloyd Dyer's attempt to delay him caused him to renew his haste. He barged into the safety bar of the side door. It swung outward under the pressure.

There was no further sound from the newspaperman as both Pete and Julie rushed outside, losing themselves in the welcome darkness of the night.

53

6

I<small>T WAS</small> snowing lightly. Pete took a few quick steps down the path that ran along the end of the main school building. Then, half dragging Julie with him, he ducked into a clump of bushes.

" Hey, take it easy, Pete. We — "

" Sh-h-h-h," he cautioned softly. " Let's just sit tight here for a minute."

Peering through the foliage, they saw Lloyd Dyer silhouetted in the lighted doorway. The newsman searched into the darkness for a few seconds, then shrugged and went back inside the building.

" Pete," Julie whispered, " let — let's get away from here."

" If Dyer spills the beans about what he saw to Lieutenant Coleman," Pete said, " we'll never be able to get far enough away. I still think we should turn this box over to the police and save our skins."

" What about Gordon's skin? " Julie reminded. " He wouldn't be doing all this if he didn't have a good reason. You know Gordon that well."

" Yeah, I guess so," Pete admitted. " But he'd better have a real good reason — and I mean real good! "

They waited a couple more minutes to be sure there was no search out for them. Then they eased out of the shrubbery, cut diagonally across the campus, and headed straight on home. They went hastily and quietly, dodging snow patches and keeping as much to the shadows as was possible. The snow flurry was very light. The flakes melted almost as quickly as they reached the ground. Several times Pete and Julie ducked behind trees or hedges as automobiles approached, although the drivers would have had difficulty seeing them through the swirling snow in front of their headlights.

"We can't take any chances of being spotted by a police car," Pete explained once when Julie protested against having suddenly been dragged through a mud puddle.

"If anyone's really looking for us," Julie said logically, "they're not going to have any particular trouble finding us. We're even in the phone book, you know. Under Rogers."

Pete admitted to himself that his sister was right. He was considerably relieved when they approached their house and saw no signs of activity — nor any police car waiting out front.

"What are you going to do with the box?" Julie asked.

"Take it to my room, I guess."

"You can't do that, Pete," Julie protested. "That would be the first place anyone would look."

"Anyone? Who?"

"There's no telling. But we just have to be careful, that's all."

"Well, maybe we could hide it in the garage," Pete suggested as they were approaching the front porch.

"Say, how about in under the front steps there?" Julie suggested, pointing to the opening at the side of the broad steps. " No one would ever think to look in there."

" That's an idea," Pete admitted. " Besides, if we leave it out here, we won't have to explain to the folks what it's all about. At least, not yet." He glanced in the lighted living-room window and saw the top of his father's head showing above the back of his favorite chair.

" Then do it, Pete," Julie prompted.

Pete knelt down in the snow and stuffed the metal box in under the porch steps. He straightened up, brushing the snow from his knees.

" What now? " Julie asked.

" Guess we'd better go in," Pete said. " Doesn't look as if Gordon got away as quick as we did. But, Sis, we better not say any more about it to the folks than we have to. Remember that Lieutenant Coleman warned us. Besides, probably the whole story will be out in tomorrow morning's *Globe*."

They were just starting up the steps when the sound of labored breathing and the crunch of running feet on the snow reached their ears.

" Let's duck," Pete said quickly.

" Why? " Julie asked. " It's probably just Gordon."

Her guess was correct. Gordon sprinted out of the shadows and into the moderate glare from the living-room window of the Rogers home.

" Phew! " Gordon gasped, pulling to a stop. " I've just about had it."

" What happened? "

" What didn't happen! " Gordon exclaimed. " I think I covered your — your escape all right. Hans Ober-

heath was really giving those policemen some trouble.
I blundered along helping them. But no sooner did we
get Oberheath into Mr. Walker's office, and I was eas-
ing myself away, than Lloyd Dyer stopped me. He
asked me if I knew anything about the box he had seen
you two smuggling out of the building."

"Wow!" Pete said.

"How come he saw it, anyway?" Gordon wondered.

Julie explained quickly what had taken place.

"What did you tell him?" Pete asked. "He could
really make it tough on us, you know."

"I acted innocent and told him it could have been
your gym shoes," Gordon said. "I wasn't sure, but —"

"Gym shoes?"

"Well, the metal box is about the size of a shoe box,"
the tall boy said.

"That was quick thinking, Gordon," Julie complimented. "And I have seen shoe boxes that were almost
that same green color. Only I don't think we ought to
lie about any of this stuff. Things are going to be tough
enough as is."

"I didn't lie," Gordon defended sternly. "I merely
said it could have been gym shoes."

"You think he believed you?" Pete asked.

"I don't know. He didn't push the subject. He
looked a little suspicious, perhaps, but — Say, what
did you do with the box, anyway?"

Pete told him. But when Gordon bent down to fish it
out from beneath the porch steps, Pete stopped him.

"Hold it, pal," he said. "Just leave that box right
where it is for a few minutes. There's another little bit

57

of business that we're going to take care of first. If Julie and I are going to be tangled up in something that's liable to land us in jail, we at least ought to know what it's all about. So you better give us the whole scoop on it right now, or — or, so help me, I'll take that box down and turn it over to Lieutenant Coleman. And if you think I'm kidding — "

" You wouldn't do that, Pete," Gordon interrupted. " You couldn't! Don't you understand how important it is that the box be kept a secret? At least, for a while."

" No, Gordon," Julie put in, " I'm afraid we don't understand. All we know is that we're helping to keep something hidden from the police. It's something that might be a big help to them in solving this whole mysterious business."

" And from what little I know about such things," Pete said, " we're fouling up the police work. Think they call it obstructing justice or something. Anyway, it's serious. Julie and I don't want any part of it."

" You've got to believe me, Pete, Julie," Gordon said with great concern and sincerity. " That box has nothing to do with solving the crime. Nothing."

" Then why is it so blasted important? "

Gordon exhaled slowly in a sigh of resignation. " I — I guess I'm not being exactly fair," he admitted. " Maybe I do owe you some kind of explanation."

" You bet you do," Pete said. " This thing really started brewing when you came up with the brain storm that Prof Nordland was murdered. It still looks to me as though it was an accident. Just what makes you figure there's a crime connected with it? "

" The whole setup, Pete," Gordon said. " Of course,

58

I could be wrong. I hope I am. But I don't think so. For one thing, that hydrogen cylinder business looks mighty suspicious."

"But," Julie said, "couldn't a hydrogen cylinder simply have a slow leak or something?"

"Nope." Gordon shook his head. "The nozzle would have had to be turned on nearly full in order to concentrate enough hydrogen in a short enough time to explode when it reached the level of the Bunsen burner. You see, hydrogen gas is lighter than air. It rises. The whole top part of the room would have been filled up fast. Finally the level would keep lowering until the flame from the Bunsen burner set it off."

"I still think it could have been an accident," Pete said.

"Not with Professor Nordland in the room," Gordon insisted. "There was nothing wrong with his ears. The hiss of escaping hydrogen would have been a sure giveaway. Besides, how would you account for the head injury?"

"What head injury?"

"Lieutenant Coleman said there was a wound on Professor Nordland's head that quite probably was caused by some kind of blow from behind."

"Maybe the force of the explosion blasted something at him," Julie said.

"Anything's possible," Gordon admitted with slight impatience, "but a detective has to keep eliminating the unlikely things until he arrives at some sort of solution."

"And," Pete put in, "the way things stack up, you just don't think it was likely that Prof Nordland was killed accidentally. That right? "

" That's about it," Gordon said, nodding. " And Lieutenant Coleman doesn't think so, either. He didn't say for sure, but I could tell by the way he talked and the questions he asked. Besides, there were plenty of clues."

" Like what? "

" Later, Pete."

" But what kind of screwball idea could it be, Gordon, to kill a man, then play around with a hydrogen and Bunsen burner setup like you say? " Pete scratched his head.

" To destroy evidence, of course," Gordon said. " Erase it with fire."

" Why? " Julie asked.

" Why the fire? "

" No, why the murder in the first place? Maybe Professor Nordland wasn't the most popular teacher in school, but he didn't have any enemies that I know of. Not real enemies."

" She's right," Pete said. " There was no reason for anyone to dislike Prof Nordland like that. Far as I could tell, he never really did anything much to make you feel very strongly toward him one way or another."

" He certainly was quiet," Julie agreed.

" Being quiet doesn't mean he wasn't a smart man," Gordon insisted.

" Who said it did? "

" As a matter of fact," Gordon went on, " he was a very intelligent man."

" O.K., O.K.," Pete said impatiently. " So he was a genius. That still doesn't give us any reason why someone should want to murder him."

"That probably isn't the way it was intended to be," Gordon said. "Perhaps Professor Nordland came upon the person unexpectedly. Maybe he surprised him going through his desk or something. There's evidence that the place, especially the office, had been ransacked. Probably Professor Nordland recognized the — the intruder. Another reason for the criminal to attempt erasing all evidence with fire."

"But just how many people would know enough to work that hydrogen and Bunsen burner gimmick?" Pete wondered.

"Believe me, Pete," Gordon assured, "anyone who was after Professor Nordland's secret was intelligent enough to know something about the explosiveness of hydrogen."

"Maybe so," Pete admitted. "And, speaking of secrets, there's the sixty-four-dollar question. Just what was the murderer looking for? No, don't tell me. The little green metal box."

"Exactly," Gordon said. "Although he wouldn't be looking for the box itself, but what's in it."

"Phew!" Pete said. "That's what I was afraid of. Pal, this could really get tough!"

"How's that?" Gordon asked.

"We're stupid enough to be holding onto the very thing that might solve the whole business," Pete said. "That's what."

"I'm afraid I agree with Pete," Julie said. "We have no right to be holding onto that box."

"But we have," Gordon insisted. "Believe me, we have."

61

"O.K., wise guy," Pete challenged, "you name it. What right have we?"

"I — I don't think I should go any farther, Pete," Gordon hesitated. "Even with you and Julie. The rest is a little vague right now, anyway. I've got to do some thinking. You'll just have to trust me for a while and —"

"Sure, sure," Pete said sarcastically, "we'll trust you — while we're cooling off behind bars. All right, chum, this is where Julie and I get off." He started to reach in under the steps.

"Hold it, Pete," Gordon said quickly. Then he shrugged in resignation. "All right — all right, I'll have to tell you."

"That's about the size of it," Pete said.

"You promise, though, that you'll keep it a secret?"

"Not if it's going to get us into trouble," Pete said.

"It won't. I promise."

"Then I'll promise."

"Julie?"

"You can count on me," she said. "But, br-r-r-r-r, it's cold out here. Can't we go inside and finish talking?"

"Good idea," Pete said. "Besides, we should let the folks know we're home."

"But what about the box?" Julie wondered.

"Right now I can't think of a better or safer place for it than right where it is," Gordon said. "Who would ever think to look there?"

"Who's going to look anyplace?" Pete asked.

"Can't tell," the other boy said. "You just can't tell."

"More riddles?"

"Let's go in," Julie prompted.

The three of them went around to the sun porch. They stomped their feet and brushed the slight powder of snow off each other's shoulders. Then they let themselves in the side door.

"Julie. Pete." Mrs. Rogers called from the living room. "That you?"

"Yes, Mom," Pete answered. "Gordon too."

"Who?"

"Gordon."

Pete's father appeared in the doorway that separated the dining room from the glassed-in sun porch.

"You kids are a little late, aren't you?" he asked, consulting his wrist watch. "Thought the library closed at nine?"

"We — we got tied up, Dad," Pete said weakly. He wanted to start right in and tell his father the happenings of the past hour. In the many problems he had taken to his parents, he had never found them lacking in sympathy and understanding. And they always had been helpful, as only parents could be. It seemed to Pete that he and Gordon and Julie certainly could use some understanding and some help with their present problems.

But he saw the flash of warning in Gordon's eyes.

"Is it all right if we go to my room and talk a few minutes, Dad?" Pete asked. "Gordon has some — some real hot news he wants to tell Julie and me."

"Must be important to let it go until this late hour," Mr. Rogers said, looking rather intently at them. "Especially since you've been together since about six o'clock this evening."

"It's something that just came up during the past

63

hour, Daddy," Julie said.

"Well, don't be long," Mr. Rogers said. "Tomorrow's a school day, and it's your bedtime right now."

The three of them went through the dining room and down the hallway to the rear of the house, where Pete and Julie had adjoining bedrooms. They went into Pete's room and closed the door. Gordon stopped inside and put his ear to the door.

"Don't worry about Dad," Pete said sharply. "He knows plenty of what's going on, but he's not the kind of guy who snoops to find things out."

"Sorry," Gordon apologized. "I — I guess this thing's kind of making me jumpy."

"Well, quit playing *Dragnet*," Pete said, "and let's get down to the business of your explaining why you think this whole thing happened."

"I'll try," Gordon said, sitting down stiffly on the edge of Pete's bed. "You ask the questions."

"First off," Pete said, "'cuz we haven't got too much time, let's figure that the thing happened just as you said — Prof Nordland caught someone ransacking his office. The thief, or whatever he was, got the best of the scuffle — which wouldn't be too hard, since Prof Nordland wasn't such a very rugged character. So the guy hit Prof Nordland on the head, then set up the hydrogen and Bunsen burner gimmick to start the fire and make the whole rotten business look like a laboratory accident. Right?"

"And don't forget," Gordon reminded, "that what you call the hydrogen and Bunsen burner gimmick also gave the murderer plenty of time to get away from the school area before the explosion. It would

64

take some time for the hydrogen to work down to the level of the Bunsen burner."

"Right," Julie said, nodding. "That makes sense."

"The question is still, Why?" Pete said. "You can't make me believe that the little metal box has anything in it that's worth committing murder to get. After all, Prof Nordland was just a high school science teacher. He was a quiet guy. He lived a quiet life with his wife, and —"

"Oh, dear," Julie moaned, "I hadn't thought of poor Mrs. Nordland. How horrible that this should happen to her! She's such a sweet person."

"It's rough," Pete said. "Really rough. All right, Gordon, tell me, who would possibly do away with Prof Nordland — and why?"

"I can't answer either of those, Pete," Gordon said. "Not exactly, anyway. But I think I can give you an idea of the whole thing — reasons, too, maybe. Without bragging, I was probably closer to Mr. Nordland than anyone else at Oakmont High. Right?"

"No doubt about it," Pete acceded. "You were his top A science student. Only one I know of, matter of fact."

"Whether that's got anything to do with it or not doesn't matter," Gordon said. "I liked Professor Nordland. He was really a fine man. I think he liked me some. At least, I know he trusted me. He took me pretty much into his confidence."

"You always did a lot of extra work around the lab," Julie said. "I guess you two were together up there quite a bit."

"Yeah. I — I always had the feeling," Gordon went

on, " that Professor Nordland was kind of testing me."

" Testing you for what? " Pete wondered.

" Oh, testing, I suppose, to determine whether it was safe to take me into his confidence."

" Why? "

" Well, I didn't know until about three weeks ago," Gordon said thoughtfully. " More than once Professor Nordland had indicated to me — oh, he never came right out and said it, but he indicated just the same — that there was some element of danger in his work."

" There's a certain danger in any chemistry lab," Pete said. " What with acids and gas and — "

" I don't mean that kind of danger," Gordon said.

" What do you mean? " Julie asked.

" Well," and Gordon took a deep breath. Pete sensed that the part of the story his lanky friend had been trying to hold back was on its way out now. " Well, Mr. Nordland's time wasn't entirely taken up with teaching high school science and chemistry classes. He was quite a scientist in his own right. He had his Ph.D. degree, you know. And a science doctorate is not easy to get. He was an ex-college professor too."

" Get to the point," Pete prompted.

" I believe Professor Nordland was carrying on some type of Government research on the side."

" You — you mean splitting atoms and that kind of thing? " Julie asked.

" Probably nothing quite that old-fashioned," Gordon said, managing a smile. " But possibly some sort of nuclear research, at that. Or any number of things. Quite a few schoolteachers do Government research, you know. We wouldn't have many schoolteachers if all the good scientists were working in Government labs. Any answer, especially in something as complicated as nuclear physics, has to be arrived at through an enormous amount of research and testing. It takes a lot of little parts to make up the whole. Intelligent scientists all over the country contribute their findings to the over-all picture."

" That's news to me," Pete said. " Does the Government know who these people are? "

" Of course," Gordon said. " The Government gives some of them direct assignments. Some just sort of freelance, hoping to come up with something that will benefit mankind."

" Like the hydrogen bomb? " Pete said.

" Take it easy, Pete," Julie scolded. " Gordon, what kind of work was Professor Nordland doing? "

" I wouldn't know, Julie," Gordon said. " But I think he had been working quite some time toward a particular discovery. And it must have been a very important piece of research."

" What makes you think that? " Pete asked.

" Because I believe he found it," the other boy said. " The way he had been acting the past week or so convinced me. He was both cheerful and cautious."

" Meaning what? " Pete asked.

" Well, to me it meant that he was cheerful over having completed his research or made his discovery," Gordon said. " And he was cautious for fear that something might happen to his discovery, or to him — or both."

" He shouldn't have kept it if he was worried about it," Pete said.

"I think he was about to get rid of it," Gordon said. "I think he was just about ready to turn the results over to our Government."

"Wow," Pete said, "you're doing a lot of supposing. Suppose you tell us what makes you think he had discovered something really important — important enough to get him killed?"

"That's simple," Gordon said levelly. "I think it's in the tin box."

"The box!" Pete exploded. "You — you mean that box is radioactive and — and — " He began brushing frantically at his clothes, as though trying to get rid of some unseen foe.

"Don't be ridiculous," Gordon scolded. "Anything that Professor Nordland might have discovered would be in the form of figures or formulas. He wasn't actually monkeying around splitting atoms or anything like that. We're certainly not equipped for anything of that nature here at Oakmont. But all those things — and the thousand and one other phases of science, nuclear or otherwise — have to be figured out first before they can be tested. That, I think, was what Professor Nordland was doing on the side."

"And you think he hit upon some big deal, huh?" Pete asked. "Atoms or no atoms."

"I don't know what other reason he would suddenly have for giving me the box," Gordon said.

"You think the secret formula is in the box?" Julie asked.

"That's what he said," Pete reminded.

"But I'm only guessing," Gordon said. "You two insisted on an explanation. I'm trying to give you the

68

best I can. I may be all wrong."

" It sounds pretty good to me," Pete said.

" Only why would Mr. Nordland give the box to you, Gordon? " Julie asked. " After all, you're just a student. It doesn't seem very smart to give a high school student such a responsibility."

" As I look back," Gordon said thoughtfully, " Mr. Nordland seemed to give the impression that something or someone was trying to get the discovery away from him. He seemed watchful and kind of fidgety."

" Did he ever tell you he was in danger? " Pete asked.

" Not exactly. He didn't talk any more than he had to, you know. But just little hints and the — well, the kind of watchful way he began to act. Then one day he seemed especially wary. That was the day he asked me if I would keep the tin box in my section of the sink cabinet."

" But why didn't he give the box to Mrs. Nordland to keep? " Julie wondered. " If anything happened to Professor Nordland, certainly Mrs. Nordland should be the one to know what to do."

" That's exactly it, I suppose," Gordon said. " Anyone after the secret would try to get it first from Professor Nordland, then from his wife."

" You don't think she knows anything about it? " Pete asked incredulously.

" I can't answer that, Pete," Gordon said. " I'd only be making a bum guess. All I know is that Professor Nordland gave me the box a couple of weeks ago."

" A couple of weeks ago," Pete said. " Where've you been keeping it? "

" I've never moved it. It has always been tucked toward the back of the cabinet under my work sink."

" Holy smoke! " Pete exclaimed. " You — you've been hiding Government secrets in your sink cabinet?"

" Don't be so dramatic, Pete," Julie scolded. " We're only guessing that there's anything other than scraps of useless paper in that box."

" Julie's right," Gordon said. " But whatever is in there is something Professor Nordland must have figured that no one would search the students' cabinets to find. He explained that to me. It was really his last indication to me that there was danger around. But certainly not to me. No one was going to bother connecting me in any way with Professor Nordland's research."

" Well, I just hope you're right, Gordon," Pete said. " And where does it all leave us right now? Somehow, Julie and I seem to have gotten involved. What about the box? "

" That's the important item now, Pete," Gordon said. " I promised Professor Nordland that under no circumstances would I surrender that box to anyone — anyone, that is, except one particular person."

" Who? " It came out of Pete in a sort of gurgle.

" I don't know." Even Gordon sounded somewhat lost. " He said I'd know when the proper time came."

THE rest of the family were already at breakfast in the dinette by the time Pete made his appearance the following morning.

" Hi, Son."

" Hi, Dad. Mom."

" Morning, dear," Mrs. Rogers said. " You're a little late getting up, aren't you? "

" Didn't sleep too well last night," Pete explained.

" I don't wonder," Mr. Rogers said cryptically.

Pete glanced quickly over at Julie. He saw the warning look that flashed in her eyes. Then he saw the morning *Globe* lying open on the china shelf. He saw the large headlines:

MYSTERY SURROUNDS DEATH OF TEACHER

He started to reach for the newspaper, then changed his mind. No point in drawing attention to the subject. After all, Lieutenant Coleman had asked them not to say any more about the affair than was absolutely necessary. It didn't prove just that simple, however.

" Quite an edition of the *Globe* this morning," his father said by way of wedging the subject into the conversation with a minimum of clumsy preliminaries. " I don't suppose there's any reason why your father and mother should be informed of just what you kids have been up to."

71

Pete swallowed uncomfortably. Although his parents usually knew pretty well what he and Julie did, there had never before been the need to pry information out of them. Pete sensed his father's mixture of exasperation and disappointment that he had not been informed about last night's occurrence until he had opened up the morning *Globe*.

"I — I'm sorry, Dad," Pete apologized. "But Lieutenant Coleman asked us to talk about it just as little as we could — at least until the story came out in the papers."

"We weren't sure it would be in this morning's paper, Father," Julie said, picking up the *Globe*, "or we certainly could just as well have told you about it last night."

"The children did right," Mrs. Rogers established her position in her children's defense. "If they were asked by the police not to talk about it, and if there was no harm to come from their silence, then they did just right."

"Yes, I suppose so," Mr. Rogers said, relaxing his face into a smile. "But if there's anything you want to add to the newspaper story, feel free to do so now. It's just possible that your mother and I might be of some help if things get too bad. And if I can read anything between the lines of this newspaper story, this whole deal is a long way from being finished."

"I — I wouldn't doubt it, Dad," Pete said. "I thought the explosion was an accident. One of those odd breaks that sometimes happen. But the way the police are going at it, and Gordon, too — well, they're handling it as though it was — was murder."

"I gather that from Lloyd Dyer's write-up, too," Mr. Rogers said. "Julie, let Pete read the story in the *Globe*."

Julie handed her brother the paper.

The story was pretty basic. Pete, Julie, and Gordon shared portions of the spotlight, with Gordon getting the fuller glare. The account was straight, the way Gordon would have told it to Lieutenant Coleman. Yet there was something of an undertone to it all that puzzled Pete, although he was unable to pin down just what it was. Lloyd Dyer didn't say it in so many words, but there was a tinge of suspicion concerning just what type of research Professor Nordland had been doing, and, beyond that, whether it had been to the best interest of the community — or the country.

Pete decided that he would pump Gordon for an explanation at his first opportunity. He had no intention of getting mixed up in any kind of political intrigue, particularly anything that might smatter of subversion.

"Anything to add to the story, Pete?" Mr. Rogers asked after Pete had laid down the paper. "I'm not asking just to be nosey, Son. I want to give you kids every opportunity to get things off your chest. If you can handle it, fine. But if you can't, your mother and I don't want to feel guilty of not offering our help. Follow me?"

"We sure do, Dad," Pete said sincerely. "And we appreciate it. But I don't think there's anything to add to Dyer's newspaper story. Not right now, anyway. Goodness knows what's going to happen from here on out."

"Well, if you get in any kind of trouble, I hope you know whom to come to."

"Golly, yes, Dad," Pete said, feeling even a little extra proud of his parents right at that moment.

"You children get at your breakfast," Mrs. Rogers prompted. "You'll have to be leaving for the police station before long."

"Police station?"

"Mr. Walker called a while ago," Julie explained. "Said we were excused from school this morning in order to keep our date with Lieutenant Coleman down at the police station. Remember? He said ten o'clock."

"That's right," Pete said. "Almost forgot. Sure wish there was some way out of it."

"There isn't," Mrs. Rogers said. "But there's no reason to worry about it, either. After all, you are not on trial. All you need to do is tell the truth. Right?"

"Right, Mom," Pete said. But, strangely, he didn't feel as coolly confident as he wished.

The reason for his uneasiness became apparent a half hour later when Gordon whistled from outside. Julie slipped into her coat, and Pete zipped up his Windbreaker. They found Gordon out front acting very strangely. He kept moving from position to position, pausing at each place and squinting toward the front steps.

"What's the deal?" Pete asked.

"Just making certain that no one can see the box you hid under there last night," Gordon explained. "Good hiding place, all right. We'll leave it there."

"Leave it there?" Julie said. "Then why have you got it under your arm?"

74

Gordon smiled. " Ha! It fooled you, too, huh? Good. Then it should work on Lloyd Dyer, if he gets curious."

" O.K., O.K.," Pete said impatiently. " I can see now that it isn't the tin box. So what? "

" Looks like it, though, doesn't it? " Gordon said, satisfied. " About the same size, and not too far off the dark-green color."

" Well, it wouldn't take any genius to tell the two apart, now that I see it better," Julie said. " Looks like a shoe box."

" It is a shoe box," the tall boy said. " Found it in our garage. Look, Pete, if Lloyd Dyer happens to be at the police station this morning, and if he brings up the subject of that green box he saw you sneaking out of the school with last night, make him think that you were just taking your gym shoes home."

" You mentioned that last night," Pete said, " and it doesn't make any more sense this morning. Especially since I haven't taken my gym shoes home once all year and had no reason to last night. On top of that, if I were carrying gym shoes, why would Julie and I have been in such a frantic hurry when Dyer called down the stairs to us? Gordon, this is too doggone crazy."

" It's the best we can do, Pete," the other boy insisted. " I tried to think of something better last night. No soap. Anyway, Dyer may not ask, especially in front of Lieutenant Coleman. Newspaper guys are often funny that way. They're always after exclusive scoops."

" In the meantime what am I supposed to do, carry this box around with me? " Pete wanted to know.

" Naw, leave it here — maybe on your back porch.

75

Then if Lloyd Dyer really wants to press the issue, it will be right there where he can see it."

"Well, I guess it's better than nothing," Pete conceded. "Of course, we could get some sense in our heads and turn the real box over to the police."

"Let's not go into that again, Pete," Gordon said. "I thought we decided about that last night."

"You decided."

"Pete," Julie spoke up, "we agreed to do it Gordon's way. He knows more of what it's all about."

"Yeah, we agreed last night," Pete admitted, "but things don't look just the same to me this morning."

"What's changed, Pete?" Gordon asked.

"What the *Globe* write-up said, that's what."

"Mr. Dyer made it sound as though maybe Professor Nordland was — er, subversive or something," Julie put in. "I think that's what Pete means."

"Yeah, that's right. What about it, Gordon?" he looked straight into his friend's eyes.

The light-haired boy turned noticeably pale. "I — I don't think Lloyd Dyer had any business to put that in the paper," he said firmly.

"But when you come right down to it, Gordon," Pete said, "just what do we know about Prof Nordland? He was always very quiet and — well, no one around Oakmont really knew him."

"I knew him," Gordon insisted.

"How well?"

"Well enough to know that he was no foreign spy or anything like that," Gordon said with some irritation. "Professor Nordland was as good an American as any of us."

" I thought he came from Europe? "

" He did. After World War II. Some of our top scientists now in this country came to America after World War II. It was their first opportunity to get out from under the oppression of dictators."

" Weren't some of them our enemies during the war? " Julie asked.

" Sure. Most of them didn't have much choice until after the surrender of their power-crazed leaders — like Hitler and Mussolini and — well, the whole bunch of them."

" How do you know so much? " Pete challenged.

" When did you read your history book last? " Gordon said.

Pete didn't answer.

" Some of America's finest rocket and jet experts are from other countries," Gordon went on. " They came over here voluntarily to live and to work. We have them to thank for some of our finest inventions and improvements. Their loyalty is to America. Far as I'm concerned that makes them Americans. Professor Nordland was one of them."

Gordon's fervor on the subject discouraged any further questions from Pete, although there were several that he might have asked.

" Pete — Julie," Gordon said, as though knowing what was on both their minds, " I'll stand by what I said last night. If any trouble comes from hiding that box, I'll take the full blame. And, believe me, if things weren't exactly as they are, I wouldn't be taking the chance, either. Or if I had to do any guessing about what was the right thing to do. But Professor Nordland

77

had briefed me so well that everything just seems to fall into its proper niche. It — it's almost as though it was all rehearsed."

"You mean even to — to his being killed?" Julie said incredulously.

"I think he merely knew he was in danger," Gordon explained. "And that's what makes whatever is in the box that much more important — and also makes it that much more important to follow his directions."

"You mentioned that someone was supposed to call for the box," Pete said. "Is that right?"

"Something like that," Gordon said. "At least, Professor Nordland said I'd know the proper time to bring it out of hiding. I — I even have a password."

"A password?" Julie said eagerly. "You didn't mention it before. What is it?"

"I can't tell you that," Gordon said.

"I want to ask one question, pal," Pete said. "What if that someone who calls for the box turns out to be a Communist or something?"

"We just wouldn't turn the box over to him," Gordon said simply.

"But how would we know?" Julie asked.

"Well, you can be mighty sure that, unless we're satisfied about the person, we won't go through with the deal. I'm sure Professor Nordland thought of that possibility; otherwise there wouldn't have been the need to be so careful. Jeepers, I'm not crazy. I'll be careful. We can't know all the answers already. We've got to go along with Professor Nordland's instructions until the whole thing jells, or until Professor Nordland's work is proved to be detrimental or dangerous.

78

Believe me, despite my feeling toward Professor Nordland, I haven't tossed out that possibility entirely."

Pete had been watching his friend closely. He had been listening carefully to every word. He was satisfied.

" O.K., pal," he said, " you sure give it the old college try. You're not a good enough actor not to have strong reasons for it. Matter of fact, it begins to make some sense. I'll call off my dogs now and go along with you. But I had to be sure."

" I'm sure now, too," Julie said. " I'm with you."

" Thanks," Gordon said fervently. " You know, you two really control this whole business anyway. You could blow it up in my face any time you want simply by going to Lieutenant Coleman and telling him the whole story."

" One explosion is enough for a while," Pete said. " And I'm beginning to believe that having the tin box wouldn't be of any particular help to the police anyway. At least I'm trying to convince myself."

" I can practically guarantee it, Pete," Gordon said.

" It's nine thirty," Julie consulted her wrist watch. " We'd better be getting down to the police station. It'll all work out, Gordon. Don't worry."

He smiled his appreciation for her confidence.

" Yeah, don't worry," Pete said. " Ha! Ha! "

THERE was little conversation between them as they walked downtown. Gordon, in particular, remained deep in thought most of the way. Having reached the point where so much depended upon their friend's brain power, both Pete and Julie respected his silence.

Although the sun was chewing away at the thin snow blanket, there was enough nip in the air to make their coats and jackets feel good. As they approached the civic center, there seemed to be a little more animation to the activity going on around them than would be caused simply by the brittleness of the temperature.

All around them people were gathered in various-sized groups. Even from a distance it was apparent that the conversations were too excited and spirited merely to be passing the time of day. Nor were the three young people unaware of the many glances that were directed toward them.

Oakmont City was a medium-sized town of something less than 7,000 population. Its streets were tree-lined and clean. Its homes had the reputation of being neatly landscaped and freshly painted. The uptown shops were mostly small and friendly. Even its super-markets and chain stores had an unusual warmth. There was a trash can on each downtown corner of Oakmont City, blue with orange lettering, which merely said, "PLEASE." The people of Oakmont City used the trash cans. They also attended P.T.A. meetings, supported the Boy Scouts, the Camp Fire Girls, and other youth groups, and turned out in force for the summer concerts in the park.

Oakmont City residents were ambitious but contented, friendly and proud, trustful yet vigilant. Pete would call them solid citizens.

But now they seemed a little flustered and definitely concerned. Oakmont City had a fine record of being rather a crime-free community. There was even a minimum of minor traffic violations. Youthful vandalism was seldom heard of. Still, it was not completely a whitewashed town; the Oakmont police would admit the existence of some cases of robbery, fraud, or other crime.

Yet, all in all, the Oakmont City law enforcement detail had little work to do, crime-wise.

But now the rumblings of a mystery were growing louder and the people were determined to have the answers. An accidental death was a rare enough occurrence in Oakmont City, and would have rated a heavy amount of public concern.

A murder — and the growing storm of opinion seemed somehow to be moving in that direction — was unheard of in Oakmont City. The citizens were up in arms.

The three young people turned the corner and came in view of the city square. Its broad expanse of lawn, now brown and mostly snow-hidden, covered a major portion of the block. The thick shade trees of summer now speared stark branches into the cold sky. Tennis and croquet courts, a children's playground, and a Boy

Scout hut occupied the southwest corner of the park. North of the play area the picnic tables were spotted under the winter skeletons of the elms and maples. Freshly shoveled brick paths wound through the park, flanked on both sides by benches.

The square was the center of community activities in Oakmont City. Clustered around it were the city hall, the police station, and the courthouse to the east. The large new Veterans' Auditorium, flanked by the smaller Chamber of Commerce building and the community lodge hall, faced the town square from the north.

West of the square were the public library, the county hospital, solid old St. Matthew's Church, and the Women's Club. The park was bordered on the south by Main Street. Convenient for picnickers was a supermarket, a toy shop, and several other small stores.

The three young people crossed the street in front of the Veterans' Auditorium, cut the corner of the park, then drew to a stop across the street from the police station.

" Wow! " Pete exclaimed. " Look at the crowd! " He estimated quickly that there were over a hundred people milling around on the broad steps which led to the entrances of both the courthouse and the police station.

" Look at all the cameras," Julie pointed out. " Must be mostly newspaper people."

" Where would that many come from? " Pete wondered.

" I imagine from all over the state, Pete," Gordon said. " Soon as they read Lloyd Dyer's account, which no doubt went out over the wire service, they probably came flocking in."

"Just because of an explosion in a high school chemistry lab?" Julie said dubiously.

"Lloyd Dyer didn't call it just an explosion," Pete corrected, recalling the *Globe* story. "Even if he doesn't know all that Gordon does about it, he didn't leave much doubt that he figured it was murder."

"It wasn't exactly his idea," Gordon said. "Lieutenant Coleman had it figured that way first."

"And you had it figured even before Lieutenant Coleman," Julie said.

"Which, as far as I'm concerned," Pete added, "leaves us right in the middle of a big mess."

As they emerged from the shrubbery at the edge of the park, they were spotted by the crowd on the courthouse steps. Photographers grabbed up their cameras, and reporters surged across the street to intercept them.

"You the kids who discovered the body?"

"Who do you think did it?"

"Which one of you is Gordon Newhall?"

"How about a statement for the Center City *Chronicle?*"

"Just a minute, kids. Hold it."

The action was as rapid as it was confusing. Flash bulbs popped in their faces, and the reporters yelled in their ears. Pete stopped a moment to smile into a camera. Julie started to dig her comb out of her purse. Gordon's face turned red to the ears as he kept on walking toward the police station.

But the newsmen weren't so easily disposed of. They formed a veritable barricade as they crowded around the three young people, popping questions and flashing cameras all the time.

"Well, the way I see it — " Pete's resistance to the attention began to falter. "The way I sum it all up is — "

"Pipe down, Pete," Gordon spoke back over his shoulder. "You know what Lieutenant Coleman said."

"What about you, Miss?" a reporter switched his interest to Julie. "You were there. What about the woman's-eye view of murder?"

Julie flinched at the word. "I — I haven't anything to say."

Just when the pressure was becoming the greatest, and Pete was having his most difficult time to refrain from making "statements," four Oakmont City police came hurrying down the steps to their rescue.

"All right, folks," a sergeant spoke up loudly as he wedged through the crowd toward the three young people, "you'll have to wait around for an official statement. These kids have been told not to talk about it."

Pete shrugged and looked helplessly at the newsmen, hoping they would not write anything against his co-operation with the press. There was no telling where he might be going to college next year and he didn't want to be preceded by bad publicity.

"You kids come on," one of the policemen instructed as the four uniformed men positioned themselves to run interference. "Lieutenant Coleman is waiting for you."

The newsmen and photographers followed them up the steps and part way into the station. They peeled off as the police-escorted trio were led straight on into the inner sanctum of the chief of detectives.

"Well, you're almost on time." Lieutenant Coleman glanced up as the group entered.

"We — we were held up a little by all the newspapermen outside," Gordon explained.

"I see," the detective said, nodding. "Well, I hope you didn't spill any beans. Those people have their jobs to do, but we're not in a position just yet to make any positive statements to the press. And when that time comes, this office will be the one to do the talking. Do you understand that?" There was a firmness in the detective's words that Pete recognized as no bluff.

"Yes, sir," Julie said.

"We're not saying anything," Gordon substantiated.

"Me too," Pete added.

"Good. Now we'll get down to business. You'd better sit down. This may take a little while. There are chairs right behind you."

The three turned and sucked in their breath in unison as they came face to angry face with, of all people, Mr. John Zucco, teacher of Chemistry I and other freshman science classes at Oakmont High.

Pete wondered immediately why Mr. Zucco would be at the police station. He looked fit to be tied, which, for Mr. Zucco, wasn't too unusual. He was a short, stocky man. Pete guessed him to be in his mid-forties. He wore a bridge of four upper front teeth. Everyone in school knew it was a bridge, for it sometimes threatened to fall out of Mr. Zucco's mouth when the science teacher became particularly angry, which was not so very infrequent. The bridge rated its full share of campus jokes and wise observations — always, however, in Mr. Zucco's absence.

Mr. Zucco's bristly gray hair stood straight out like a frightened Hottentot's — at least, the fringe that circled the bald spot on top. By reputation Mr. Zucco was a skilled scientist, and he certainly looked the part of the classic movie version of a scientist. Despite his almost comic appearance and his frequently strange actions, Mr. Zucco seemed dedicated to his pursuit of learning in the fabulous world of science.

Mr. Zucco was normally a quiet man, although the lava of his fiery temper always seemed to be seething just beneath the surface of his outer actions. His occasional outbursts of temper hardly endeared him to the hearts of the student body. Besides that, his assignments and examinations were rated the hardest at Oakmont High.

He had grown even more taciturn after Professor Nordland had arrived at Oakmont High and been appointed head of the science department. Having taught at Oakmont for two years prior to Professor Nordland's appearance, Mr. Zucco had expected to get the promotion. What had been against him, his dour personality, his toughness as a teacher, or what, was a point of conjecture among the students.

From the first day of Professor Nordland's arrival, Mr. Zucco had done little to hide his disappointment at not receiving the appointment as department head. He'd shown no friendship toward Professor Nordland, and never spoke to the younger man except on pressing school business matters. And then it was always with red-faced courtesy on Mr. Zucco's part.

" Hello, Mr. Zucco," Pete managed, once he was sufficiently over his surprise.

The science teacher merely grunted impatiently and folded his fattish arms across his wrinkled coat front. It occurred to Pete then that there could be but a choice of two reasons for Mr. Zucco to be there at the police station. Either he knew something about the case of Professor Nordland's strange death that would be of help to the police or he was under some sort of suspicion.

Gordon had paused also, and stood staring wordlessly at the chubby Italian scientist. For no particular reason that Pete could figure, Gordon's face had turned an ash-gray color. Pete had seen him that way on other occasions. Usually just preceding some strange event. Pete would have given anything at the moment to know just what was going on inside his friend's head.

For the first time Pete noticed Lloyd Dyer seated in the rear corner of the medium-sized office. The newsman got up to offer Julie his seat.

" Hi, Pete," Dyer said, slipping Pete his usual wink of encouragement. The newspaperman's expression gave no indication that he was at all interested in the reason Pete and Julie had been in such a hurry to get out of the school building with the green metal box the night before. Pete was greatly relieved. Evidently Dyer had given no significance to the box.

One other familiar figure was in Lieutenant Coleman's office. It was Hans Oberheath, the part-time janitor. Hans was a wizened little man about whom little was known other than that he was seen brooming his way around the school most any time of the day or evening.

Hans looked worried too. Pete had an idea that the school janitor had undergone quite a session of questioning since his involuntary appearance last night between the two policemen, while Pete and Julie were smuggling the tin box out of the school building.

Getting any information out of Hans Oberheath would be no simple task. As far as anyone could make out, the little man was stone deaf. Nor could Pete recall ever having heard him speak over a half-dozen words at any one time. Strictly a recluse, Hans lived alone in a little shack on the northern outskirts of Oakmont City. Loneliness had not been good for Hans Oberheath. He was old beyond his years, haggard appearing, with a shuffling, stoop-shouldered gait. About the only things in the hermitlike man's favor were that he did his school janitoring well, and was an avid reader, making frequent trips to and from the public library.

Looking at him now, Pete recognized the same sort of wildness in the man's eyes that he had seen staring up at him from the darkness at the foot of the stairs during last night's hectic episode in the school building.

Why had Hans ducked back into the darkness? Why hadn't he come upstairs to investigate the activity which was certainly out of place in the school building and at that time of night? Also, he must have felt the explosion, even if he couldn't hear it. No, Hans Oberheath's actions just didn't make sense to Pete.

Now the little man flashed him a twisted smile of recognition. It could have meant anything — or nothing.

Lieutenant Coleman shoved some papers aside on his desk, and turned his attention to the gathering. "This case has all the earmarks of coming to a fast windup," he announced, directing his conversation particularly toward Gordon, Pete, and Julie. "Due to some good fortune and some fast work on the part of you kids in putting out the fire, certain carelessly left clues — or, shall we say, possible clues — have come to light. Had the fire gone unchecked, as was no doubt intended, all evidence would have been destroyed, not to estimate how much of the school building."

"Clues?" Pete whispered involuntarily.

"That's right," Lieutenant Coleman said, nodding. "Primarily fingerprints."

"Whose fingerprints?" Julie asked.

"We'll get to that in time," the detective chief said. "Now you three probably are aware that no great friendship existed between Mr. Zucco and Professor Nordland. Am I correct in making that assumption?"

Their very silence seemed answer enough to Lieutenant Coleman, and he didn't pursue the question, but went on to another. "All of you take science classes. Gordon, you and Pete had classes under Professor Nordland. Julie, you take first-year chemistry under Mr. Zucco. Am I correct?"

They nodded their heads in assent. Pete was slightly amazed at how Lieutenant Coleman could already toss such facts around as though he were vice-principal or something. Nor did Pete miss the friendliness with which the detective called them by their first names.

But the next question was not quite so casual. "Now," Lieutenant Coleman went on, "I want you to think this over carefully. But when you answer, I want the truth, regardless of personalities involved. Understand? "

" Yes, sir."

" I do."

" Yep."

" Good. Now, we're all aware that there is no law dictating that two people must like each other. Enmities, large and small, are common items, and are of no real significance in themselves. However, what is of some significance is this: Do any of you recall any recent differences between the two men? perhaps in the form of an argument? "

The room was very quiet. What Lieutenant Coleman implied was obvious. The lid was off, and suspicion leaped up like a jack-in-the-box. For the first time it occurred to Pete that Mr. Zucco's dislike for Professor Nordland might have been more than the common garden variety of professional jealousy.

But Pete certainly didn't recall any recent unusual events taking place between the two teachers. Even if he did, he wasn't at all sure that he would have been brave enough to mention them at the moment. The situation was becoming extremely serious. The outright accusation that was hidden only shallowly behind the detective's question was far too evident not to be frightening.

He saw too that Julie had no intention of answering.

Then he heard the funny noises in Gordon's throat. The ash-gray color was back again in his face. His hands were clutching nervously at his knees.

" What is it, Newhall? " Lieutenant Coleman prompted. " Did you see or hear the two men arguing

90

recently, or anything like that? "

" Ye-yes, sir," Gordon was having trouble.

" Out with it, boy," the detective said, leaning forward anxiously. " What did you see? "

" I didn't see it, sir. I just heard it."

" All right, all right. What did you hear? "

" I — I heard Mr. Zucco threaten Professor Nordland."

Julie gasped, and Pete stared at Gordon in disbelief. What kind of business was Gordon trying to pull? Or was he telling the truth?

" You say threaten? " Lieutenant Coleman also seemed taken aback by the sudden bluntness of Gordon's statement.

" Yes, sir."

" When? "

" Yesterday afternoon."

" Where? "

" In — in Professor Nordland's office just off the chemistry lab."

" Where were you? " Lieutenant Coleman snapped out the questions as fast as Gordon could answer them.

" I — I was getting a book out of the cabinet under my assigned lab sink," Gordon explained. His voice was low, almost as though he were talking to himself, thinking out every word before he uttered it.

Pete realized suddenly that his friend was telling the absolute truth. He couldn't imagine why Gordon hadn't mentioned it earlier. But the other boy had been quite secretive all the way; so perhaps he had just been waiting for the right moment — this moment — to reveal it.

" What did you hear, son? " Lieutenant Coleman

91

said, struggling for calmness. " What exactly? "

There wasn't a breath drawn, not a movement made in the entire room.

" I — I heard Mr. Zucco tell Professor Nordland that someday he might be very sorry that he ever had come to Oakmont High."

A bushel of dynamite sticks could have caused only slightly more of an explosion than the sudden violence created by Gordon Newhall's statement.

Lieutenant Coleman's fist came down on the desk. At the same moment a chair crashed over backward, as Mr. Zucco leaped to his feet and, with a frenzied roar, sprang at Gordon.

CHAPTER

9

PETE admitted afterward that it was mostly reflex action on his part. His training in athletics had given him a speed of muscle that, on occasions, outstripped his speed of thought.

As the enraged Mr. Zucco charged past him, intent on getting to Gordon, Pete simply shoved out his foot. The science teacher tripped over it and crashed to the floor. In a flash Lieutenant Coleman was upon him. He lifted the protesting man to his feet. Mr. Zucco nearly burst a blood vessel in a rather poor attempt to subdue his violent temper. But whatever demonstration he might have resorted to was quickly dampened by the firm grip of the detective.

" Shall we figure that as a confession of guilt, Mr.

Zucco? " Lieutenant Coleman queried. " Are you ready to tell us the whole story? "

Seeming to realize suddenly that his quick rage had hurt only himself, the science teacher clenched his fists and forcibly brought his temper under control. Pete watched the flaring redness in his face subside to its normal tint. Mr. Zucco relaxed and turned toward him.

" Thank you, young man," he said, " for — for tripping me. I'm afraid my temper isn't one of my assets."

" I would say that it's your undoing," Lieutenant Coleman said. " It is probably the same temper that is responsible for Professor Nordland's death."

The science teacher's eyes widened. " You — you don't actually believe I killed Nordland? " he said.

" So far it figures," the detective said.

" That's ridiculous. Absolutely ridiculous," Mr. Zucco protested, as redness began to creep back into his cheeks. " I'll admit that I felt no particular friendliness toward Professor Nordland. But I deny hating him. And I most emphatically deny having anything to do with violence toward my former associate."

" Do you also deny what young Newhall here just said about your threat to Professor Nordland in his office yesterday? " Lieutenant Coleman asked.

" Perhaps the boy heard it," Mr. Zucco admitted, " but he didn't hear it exactly correctly. And he most certainly misinterpreted it."

" All right, let's have your interpretation," the detective invited.

" As you may know," Mr. Zucco said carefully, " Professor Nordland was not in the best of health. That's the primary reason why he left teaching in a university out on the Coast and came here to Oakmont City. Doctors had recommended a change of climate."

" Do you know the nature of his illness? " the detective asked.

" He never said exactly, and I never asked," Mr. Zucco said. " It was a respiratory ailment of some kind. Bronchial, I believe. Lately it had been a little aggravated. Yesterday afternoon when we were talking in his office he coughed a few times. I said something about how he might be sorry that he had come to Oakmont City. After all, he had given up a nice college professorship to come here, and he still seemed to have his cough. That's all there was to the discussion."

" How does that explanation sound to you, Gordon? " Lieutenant Coleman turned to the tall boy.

" I — I really couldn't say word for word how it did go," Gordon admitted. " I guess it's possible that I heard just that one part."

" Then Mr. Zucco's explanation could be correct," the detective assumed.

" I guess it could be," Gordon said. But Pete could tell by the dubious expression on his friend's face that he wasn't satisfied with Mr. Zucco's interpretation.

" There's another little item," the science teacher went on with renewed confidence, "that might have some bearing on this whole business. Much as I dislike talking about a person who is no longer able to defend himself, I feel it's my duty to mention my suspicion that Professor Nordland was not confining his activities to teaching high school sciences."

" Go on," Lieutenant Coleman encouraged.

"I often wondered if Professor Nordland was not conducting experiments on the side which were not to the best interests of our country," Mr. Zucco said flatly.

"I don't believe that!" Gordon exclaimed.

"Continue, Mr. Zucco," Lieutenant Coleman invited, scowling at Gordon's outburst. "Are you trying to say that Professor Nordland was a subversive — perhaps working for some unfriendly power?"

"I don't wish to make any direct accusations," the high school teacher said. "I only say that certain experiments and certain fragments of formulas which I caught occasional brief glimpses of had nothing to do with the high school science we teach here at Oakmont High."

Pete looked at Gordon. The tall boy's eyes shifted around the room without focusing on any particular objects. Pete sensed that even Gordon was faltering a little in his blind loyalty to Professor Nordland.

What if Mr. Zucco's suspicions proved well founded? What if Professor Nordland had been an agent for some foreign power? It would have been simple for him to give Gordon the impression that he was conducting part-time research in behalf of the United States. He might even have been interested in gradually indoctrinating Gordon to his cause. It most certainly was not beyond possibility.

Pete suppressed a shudder. For it occurred to him suddenly that the tin box which lay hidden under his front steps might well contain material that would convict Julie and him, as well as Gordon, of some subversive crime. Perhaps even espionage.

If anything could be read into Gordon's expression,

and his obvious uneasiness, it was that his thoughts were closely paralleling Pete's.

Of course, there was no particular reason why Mr. Zucco's story had to be correct. The fact most apparent to Pete was that the case was getting more complicated with each passing minute. He noticed that Hans Oberheath had been looking more at ease as Lieutenant Coleman's attention was concentrated on Mr. Zucco.

Yet, what had Oberheath been doing in the school building at that time of night? As far as Pete knew, the janitor's customary procedure was to have his cleaning up finished by dinnertime. Could Oberheath have been working in cahoots with Professor Nordland — or against him? They were all possibilities as far as Pete was concerned.

Lieutenant Coleman continued questioning Mr. Zucco for a while, but nothing further emerged that seemed of any particular importance to Pete.

For the next ten minutes the detective directed his queries at Hans Oberheath. The results were practically nil. The questions had to be repeated loudly, and sometimes written out, before the wizened janitor seemed even to understand what the lieutenant was getting at.

" I don't think Oberheath is quite as dense as he lets on," Lloyd Dyer spoke up. " And he certainly was doing some fast and heavy protesting when the two policemen spotted him leaving the school grounds last night. They practically had to carry him back to the building. That just doesn't seem like any way for a person to act if he hasn't got some reason for it, or something to hide."

"With all due respect to Mr. Oberheath," Lieutenant Coleman said, "we have to allow for a certain amount of strange action. If he's just playing a game of possum, we'll find out in time."

"And it may be too late," Lloyd Dyer commented half to himself.

During the conversation, Pete watched Hans Oberheath's face closely. Not a flicker of an eyelid or a twitch of a muscle indicated that the janitor was in the least aware of the gist of the conversation going on between the detective and the newsman. Pete was inclined to side slightly with Lloyd Dyer, however. Even though he was willing to concede Hans Oberheath's stone-deafness, he found it difficult to accept the old man's present display of ignorance. He had seen the janitor hauling home armloads of books from the public library, and knew he was well-read. There was also an aware look in the man's eyes which belied the air of dreaminess with which he apparently surrounded himself as a protective measure. Pete believed Hans was putting on some kind of act. It was true that the janitor was a strange person. It did not follow, however, that he was ignorant. Further, Pete believed that Hans had qualified for his school job by showing a certain intelligence. Janitors as well as teachers do not simply walk in and get a school job without a certain amount of practical screening.

"Well," Lieutenant Coleman was saying, "there is not sufficient evidence against either of these men to hold them on the charge of murder. We found fingerprints of both of them in the chemistry laboratory. It was logical that the prints should be there; since both

97

readily admit having been in the lab yesterday. It becomes increasingly apparent that the prints have no value, except the slight one of circumstantial evidence."

" Then you completely discount Newhall's testimony about overhearing the argument between Zucco and Professor Nordland? " Lloyd Dyer asked, putting pencil to tablet.

" In the first place," Lieutenant Coleman said, " no one here today has testified to anything. This is not a trial, but an informal hearing. Nothing is on record. In the second place, I'm not discounting anything. The fact remains, nevertheless, that I have no evidence sufficient to hold either of these men."

" Then I assume I can leave," Mr. Zucco said.

" You can leave here," the chief detective said, " but don't try to leave town. You'll be called in again."

" Well, you just be sure you have a good reason for it," Mr. Zucco said sharply.

" There'll be a reason," the lieutenant assured.

The science teacher rose and went out the door. Hans Oberheath looked at Lieutenant Coleman.

" You can go too," the police officer said, then motioned toward the door so that Hans Oberheath would understand. The little man got up and walked out.

" Well, Lieutenant," Lloyd Dyer said, " what happens next? "

" I'm afraid that will have to come under the heading of police business, Dyer," the detective said, smiling. " But I'll let you know just as soon as things develop that we feel can be released to the press."

" Sorry I got snoopy," the reporter apologized.

"We've all got our jobs to do," Lieutenant Coleman said.

"Something is bound to break," Dyer said by way of encouragement.

"Something always does," the detective said. "In the meantime we might as well let in the rest of the reporters waiting out front. No big story to give them, but they'll want something to make their trip worthwhile."

"To a newsman a murder's always worth-while," Dyer said. "Story-wise, that is."

"There's one little item you might remember on that score," Lieutenant Coleman said. "You reporters get too anxious. Remember, this thing hasn't been pinned down as a murder. In fact, there are high possibilities that it was all an unfortunate accident."

"I'll buy that version any time you want to accept it," Lloyd Dyer said, smiling.

"But I'll not accept it," the detective said, "until we've eliminated every possible chance of its having been a crime."

"You figure that you eliminated two this morning?"

"Not by a long shot," Lieutenant Coleman said. "Not by a very long shot." Then he turned his attention to the three young people. "What about you folks? Did you get any new ideas while all the questioning was going on? You were on the scene last night. You got the first picture of the thing. If the pieces don't fall into their proper places, I want to hear about it. Young lady, what about you?"

"I — I have nothing to add, I'm afraid," Julie said self-consciously.

" Pete? "

" I'll pass," Pete said. " Things got going over my head way back there someplace."

" Gordon," the detective said, " you seem to have most of the ideas. Have you got anything to say about this morning's little tea party? "

" Not a whole lot, I'm afraid," Gordon said, " except that I think Mr. Zucco is way off base by implying that Professor Nordland was doing anything that wasn't absolutely all right."

" Do you know what he was doing, Gordon? " Lieutenant Coleman said, looking at him closely.

" No, sir."

" But you know he was doing something other than what he was being paid for doing as a high school science and chemistry teacher? "

" Well, I — I'm pretty sure he was doing some kind of outside research," Gordon said.

" Why are you sure? "

" I used to help him," Gordon said. " He sometimes had me do little parts of experiments that I knew had nothing to do with our regular school assignments."

" What kind of experiments? "

" Well, like breaking down simple compounds into their basic ingredients," Gordon said. " Or testing for traces of certain elements in other compounds or solutions. They weren't particularly complicated things. But it was all good experience for me. And Professor Nordland would always tell me just what to do."

" But you don't know why he was doing all that stuff, or why he would have you help him? "

" Gordon was Professor Nordland's star pupil," Pete

spoke up. " He's the only guy I knew of in the class who got straight A's. He earned them too. So, if Professor Nordland needed help, it was a cinch he would ask Gordon. That's only natural."

" Who's arguing? " Lieutenant Coleman said. " The question is, Why did he need the help and, more important, What was it that he needed help in? You don't know what it all added up to, is that right, Gordon? "

" Yes, sir," Gordon said. " Professor Nordland was my friend. I knew he was doing some kind of outside research. I was proud to be able to help him even a little bit. He never told me the details, and I didn't ask. But whatever he was doing was all right. I'm sure of that."

" Well, there's nothing but Mr. Zucco's rather hot-tempered opinion to indicate otherwise," the detective said. " So we'll just have to let that part of it ride until we uncover more evidence. Hey, what's the matter with you, Pete? "

Pete hadn't realized that Lieutenant Coleman's words had caused him to jerk up straight in his chair. It had been the detective's mention of uncovering new evidence that had sent Pete's thoughts flying to the tin box which still lay hidden beneath the front steps of his house. That box might well contain a great many answers to the assortment of questions that had come up that morning.

And Pete was still of the opinion that keeping it in hiding was like toying around with a short-fused stick of dynamite. But he also had a long memory for promises. And one glance at Gordon gave no indication that the other boy was relieving him of the responsibility.

"Guess — guess I got a cramp or something," Pete said, stretching elaborately.

"Well, as soon as you get rid of it," Lieutenant Coleman smiled, "you might as well beat it to school. We've done about all we can here this morning. Again I say, don't talk this around a lot. It's no secret, of course, and there'll be a lot of rumors floating around. You can't prevent that. But I prefer that you kids neither add to nor try to correct the rumors. O.K.?"

"We won't talk about it," Gordon said.

"Good. All right, Sergeant Haskins can drive you on over to school. I may be calling you down here from time to time, so don't worry about it."

"Lieutenant Coleman," Gordon said with sudden fervor, "if there's anything at all that I can do to help catch whoever's behind all this, I'll do it. Anything."

"Sure, son, I know," the detective said. "But don't let this thing get you. As I said earlier, though, we're not at all convinced that this whole unfortunate situation wasn't an accident."

"I'm convinced," Gordon said firmly. "It was no accident."

"Gordon," Pete prompted, "let's go." He stood up and took hold of his friend's arm before the other boy launched into more theories. "Coming, Julie?"

"Follow me, kids," Sergeant Haskins said. "I'll run you on over to school."

They went out the side door in order to avoid the waiting newsmen. They climbed into the white-sided squad car, Julie in front and the two boys in back. Soon they were headed toward school.

Gordon was deep in thought when Sergeant Haskins

turned and spoke over his shoulder.

"Which one of you fellows was it that called in last night?" he asked.

"I did," Pete said. "And, boy, was I scared! Bet you had a tough time making anything out of what I was saying."

"Well, I've had worse," the policeman said. "But I'm pretty fast at jotting the things down on my desk pad. Got into the habit years ago. Then I can unscramble my notes afterward. You know, I almost tabbed yours as a crank call, though. We get them once in a while. You can often sense them, and —"

"You mean you almost didn't do anything about Pete's call?" Gordon emerged from his thoughts.

"Oh, we investigate them all," Sergeant Haskins said. "But sometimes when they seem particularly phony, we give other, more urgent, things priority. If there hadn't been such excitement in your voice I might have waited until one of our patrolmen called in, then sent him over to investigate. Lieutenant Coleman was out on another job."

"Well, I'm glad you didn't wait," Pete said. "If there was anything we wanted in a hurry it was to have some policemen around."

"Say, Sergeant Haskins," Gordon said when they were still several blocks from school. "I — I wonder if you'd let us off at the next corner?"

"You kids figuring to ditch school or something?"

"No, sir," Gordon said, "but lunch period is just starting at school and — well, we'd like to make a call."

Pete glanced at his friend, but held his questions until later.

103

"Guess it's all right," the policeman agreed. "Say where."

"There at the corner will be fine," Gordon said, pointing.

The sergeant pulled the patrol car to the curb. Although Pete had been dying to question Gordon about the sudden move, he had come to realize that his neighbor friend usually had a pretty good reason for his actions, and that the best time to question them was when they were alone.

But as soon as the police car drove off, leaving the three of them standing on the sidewalk, Pete opened up.

"All right," he demanded, "give. What's this all about? We're supposed to be on our way to school — not horsing around here four blocks away."

"We're not horsing, Pete," Gordon assured.

"Then why did you have him let us out here, Gordon?" Julie asked.

"Professor Nordland's house is right around the corner," Gordon explained.

"So?" Pete asked.

"I think it might be a good idea if we called on Mrs. Nordland," Gordon said.

"Jeepers, fellow," Pete protested, "she's probably all broken up over this thing. I — I wouldn't feel right going there and — "

"She's probably very lonely," Julie cut in. "Gordon, I think it's a fine idea. She needs friends right now. We might be of some help to her."

"It might be mutual," Gordon said.

"Look, pal," Pete said, "I hope you're not figuring

104

to start asking her a lot of questions."

"I don't know," Gordon said. "We'll just have to see. All I know is that we should do anything we can to get this business straightened out. I also think we should give her some inkling of what the newspapers are going to say about Mr. Zucco accusing Professor Nordland of — of maybe working for some foreign interest. Something like that could ruin Mrs. Nordland's future, you know."

"Boy, Gordon," Pete said uncertainly, "I just don't know anything any more. Half the time I feel like I'm up to my chin in quicksand."

"Gordon," Julie said, "let's make it just a social call on Mrs. Nordland. Let's not burden her with any more problems — not right now."

"Well," Gordon said, "we'll just have to see what develops."

CHAPTER

10

Mrs. Nordland was a somewhat tall and thin lady with light hair and a fair complexion. Her cheekbones were rather prominent and her nose was as straight as a problem in arithmetic. She was very attractive, though not beautiful. She was of Nordic descent — blond and blue-eyed.

But her eyes now were reddened by grief.

"Hello," she said, opening the screen door. Her eyes settled upon Gordon. "You're Gordon Newhall, aren't you?"

"Yes, ma'am," Gordon said.

"I knew," Mrs. Nordland said, pushing at a smile. "My husband spoke of you so often that I think I would have known you if we had simply met on the street."

"Mrs. Nordland," Gordon said, seeming to have a little difficulty with his voice, "this — this is Julie Rogers, and her brother, Pete. We — we —"

"Won't you come in, please?" Mrs. Nordland invited. "I'm so glad you came to see me. And, please, don't feel uncomfortable. These things must be faced bravely. We must have faith that even such tragedies as these are all a part of our Lord's plan. I have had time to get over the first shock. I mustn't allow myself to continue grieving. Mr. Nordland wouldn't want that."

The three young people watched and listened in open admiration. Pete couldn't recall ever having liked a person so much in such a short time as he did Mrs. Nordland. She was completely genuine, putting on no false airs of any kind.

"Please sit down," she invited. "Couldn't I make some tea and a few sandwiches, or —"

"Oh, no, thank you, Mrs. Nordland," Julie said. "We have to be getting on to school pretty soon now."

"Mrs. Nordland," Gordon said, "is there anything we can do to help you? I mean, even if we're just high chool students, there must be something. My father's local merchant. Julie and Pete's father is an attorney. Our mothers too — well, I know they would all want to offer their help."

"You're very kind," Mrs. Nordland said, smiling.

106

" And if there is anything, you may be sure I shall not hesitate to call on you. And, Julie, I'm so glad you came today. I shall be wanting to talk to your father at some later date. But, you see, I have two older brothers. They're both arriving here by airplane sometime this afternoon or evening. They will help me settle whatever things must be done."

" Oh, I'm glad some of your family will be here, Mrs. Nordland," Julie said. " That's such a comfort."

" Well, Mrs. Nordland," Gordon said, starting to rise, " I guess we'd better be on our way."

" So soon? "

" Well, we just wanted to stop by and see that everything was all right with you," Gordon explained. " I considered Mr. Nordland one of my very best friends. Someday I'm going to be a chemist, you know. Mr. Nordland taught me so much."

" He was very proud of you, Gordon," Mrs. Nordland said. " He had great hopes for you. I'm certain his hopes will all bear fruit as time passes."

" Thank you, Mrs. Nordland," Gordon said.

" I'm sorry I'm not better acquainted with you other two young people," the scientist's widow said. " But I know you were both friends of my husband."

" I took freshman chemistry from Mr. Zucco," Julie said. " I really didn't know Mr. Nordland, except by sight."

Perhaps it was the mention of Mr. Zucco that set Gordon off. Perhaps it was that he had done all the hedging he could around the subject that was foremost in his mind. Regardless of what triggered his tongue, the thought blurted out.

107

"Mrs. Nordland," he said, "I — I guess you know that Professor Nordland's death was no accident."

"Gordon!" Pete protested quickly. "What's the idea? You've got no right to —"

"Please." Mrs. Nordland held up her hand to interrupt the argument. "Please. Go on, Gordon."

"I — I'm sorry," Pete said, "but Gordon has no business upsetting you with what he thinks or doesn't think."

"It is all right," Mrs. Nordland said. "Really, it — it doesn't hurt me. We have to face the facts. I think it's best that we do talk about it a little. I hadn't intended to myself, but I'm relieved that you brought it up. Several things puzzle me. Gordon, I wonder if you would be kind enough to tell me what you know, or what you suspect, about my husband's death. The police were not very thorough in their explanation. I suppose they were protecting my feelings. I appreciate that, but I must know the entire story. I'm entitled to know it, am I not?"

"Yes, ma'am," Pete said.

Gordon took a full ten minutes relating the happenings from the moment of last night's explosion to their present visit. He told how he thought Professor Nordland had been killed. But when it came to theorizing on the possible reasons, his story came to a quick close.

"Thank you very much, Gordon," Mrs. Nordland said when he had finished. "That helps a great deal. And I'm afraid I agree with your idea that my husband didn't meet an accidental death. Not that his work was absolutely foolproof — for all humans are subject to making mistakes — but none of the series of last night's happenings that led up to the final explosion of hydrogen would be the type of mistake that Mr. Nordland would make. Most certainly he would not have made them all. And how could you explain the coroner's report that Mr. Nordland's head injuries indicate that he was killed before the explosion occurred?"

"Lieutenant Coleman didn't tell us that," Pete said.

"It was pretty obvious, Pete," Gordon said.

"What was obvious about it?"

"The cabinets had protected Professor Nordland from the main force of the explosion," Gordon explained. "His clothes weren't even scorched. And, more important even, he was covered with fragments of glass and things. It would indicate that he had been lying there behind the cabinets at the time of the explosion. In which case —" Gordon stopped suddenly. He shook himself as though coming out of his thoughts. "I — I'm sorry, Mrs. Nordland," he apologized. "I'm not being very considerate."

"It's all right, Gordon," the professor's widow said. "I want to hear it all. I want to get everything straightened out as clearly as I can. You have strengthened some of my own thoughts. Now," and she looked closely into Gordon's eyes, "is there anything you've been wanting to ask me, but are refraining because of your — your consideration for me? Please don't hesitate."

Pete could see that Mrs. Nordland was completely sincere. He also knew that it was the opening Gordon had been hoping for; yet, with due respect for Mrs. Nordland's feelings, the science student hadn't felt it his part to propose the subject.

109

"Mrs. Nordland," Gordon said now, "do you know what kind of outside research your husband was doing?"

If she was surprised by the question, the scientist's widow gave no indication of it.

"You're not just guessing?" she said. "I mean, are you certain he was doing outside research?"

"I—I'm pretty sure, ma'am," Gordon said. "He took me into his confidence quite a bit. He never came right out and told me what he was doing, but he did indicate that it was secret research of some kind, and that he expected me to keep my curiosity to myself. I did, but it wasn't always easy."

"Gordon," Mrs. Nordland said, "I'm going to tell you something that may surprise you. You knew more about what my husband was doing in his field of research than I."

"But how — why — ?"

"The reason is rather simple, I'm afraid," Mrs. Nordland said. "The less I knew, the less danger I would be in."

"My goodness," Julie spoke up, "this is beginning to sound like a television mystery or — Oh, I'm sorry, Mrs. Nordland. I — I forgot myself."

"It's all right, Julie. And you are quite correct. Gordon, I hope you don't feel that Mr. Nordland was placing you in any danger. I can assure you he wouldn't."

"I had no idea the work was so serious," Gordon said thoughtfully. "So — so dangerous."

"I'm not certain it was," Mrs. Nordland said. "But I do know that my husband began to lose a lot of sleep a few months ago. I also know that he needed some help in whatever he was doing. Help, at least, in some of the smaller time-consuming details. That much he indicated to me."

"A few months ago?" Gordon mused. "That was about the time he really started letting me help him."

"That is correct. I know he spoke often of you as his student most likely to succeed in a scientific career. I believe he took great pride in helping you. Whether or not he ever mentioned it to you I don't know, but my husband was planning to sponsor your career in any way he could. As you know, we have no children of our own. Every man has a hope — a secret hope, at least — of finding someone to carry on his work when he is unable to continue. I have every reason to believe that Mr. Nordland had placed his hopes in you, although he didn't feel it his place to mention it — at least, not yet."

"That's a wonderful thing to know, Mrs. Nordland," Gordon said, blinking fast.

"And now," Mrs. Nordland went on, "I'm sure you are wondering whether the research work my husband was doing was absolutely legal and for the best interests of our country. In these times that question is almost certain to come up."

None of the three young people was able to conceal his surprise at how candidly Mrs. Nordland had brought up the subject that was of such concern to them at the moment.

"Oh, you needn't pretend," she said, mustering a smile. "A Mr. Dyer of the *Globe* telephoned this morning. He didn't come right out and ask, but I gathered that he was considering the same possibility."

" Lloyd Dyer? " Gordon said. " But he had no right to be bothering you, Mrs. Nordland. Or prying."

" I'm afraid newspaper people don't think of it as prying, Gordon," Mrs. Nordland said. " They are simply gathering news. Besides, Mr. Dyer was very pleasant, and told me not to pay any attention to whatever rumors might start circulating around about my husband's research being of a questionable nature. I was only sorry that I didn't have some evidence to furnish Mr. Dyer in order to squelch any such rumors."

" What kind of evidence, Mrs. Nordland? " Pete asked.

" Well, Mr. Dyer thought my husband might have left something in writing that might clearly prove the legality of his work."

" But he didn't? " Julie asked.

" I've been unable to find anything in the papers we have here at the house," Mrs. Nordland said. " I'm afraid Mr. Nordland was so occupied with his work that he never thought of leaving anything like that. Although he seemed restless recently, I don't believe he suspected that anything serious would happen to him. I'm not aware of what he did with the results of his experiments. I don't imagine he told you, either, Gordon."

The bespectacled boy didn't answer.

Of course, Pete thought immediately of the tin box, and wondered why Gordon didn't mention it. Probably that box contained all the evidence needed to prove or disprove Mr. Nordland's loyalties.

" Chances are he mailed or delivered his findings at intervals to his superiors," Mrs. Nordland went on. " I suppose you young people realize that quite a few schoolteachers do part-time research for our Government. Others do experimenting and tests for various business firms that are too small to afford their own testing laboratories."

"Gordon mentioned something about that," Pete said. "I really don't know much about that stuff myself."

"Mrs. Nordland," Gordon said, "we really have to get to school now. I'm sure that whatever Professor Nordland did was one hundred per cent all right."

"If it wasn't, we're all liable to be in some trouble," Pete said, pretty much without realizing how it sounded.

"Pete, you be quiet," Julie scolded.

"I'm confident you needn't worry," Mrs. Nordland said.

"I'm sure too," Gordon agreed. "Well, Mrs. Nordland, if there's anything at all we can do, please call us."

"I will," she said, "and thanks so much for stopping by. You've made me feel a whole lot better. And you've cleared up some points in my mind. And please don't wait for me to call. Stop in any time. I — I'm afraid the next few days won't be easy."

Pete saw the grief start to creep back into her face and eyes. It made him realize how bravely she had been conducting herself during the past fifteen minutes. They said their good-bys and started toward school.

They had walked less than two blocks when a tan coupé pulled up beside them.

"Well, you kids are just lucky I'm not a truant officer," Lloyd Dyer said, grinning from behind the steering wheel. "I thought Sergeant Haskins took you to school a half hour or so ago."

"It was lunch period," Gordon said, "so we stopped in to see Mrs. Nordland."

"Oh? Well, that was a good idea. I talked to her this morning on the phone. She seems very nice."

"She is," Julie said.

"Well, come on, hop in," the reporter invited. "I'm going over to the school myself. Want to scout around a bit and talk to Mr. Walker. Maybe uncover a clue or two. You know, this thing isn't getting any less complicated by the minute. Too many things don't quite add up. There might even have been some basis to Zucco's accusation this morning that Professor Nordland could have been up to something he shouldn't have."

"I don't think so," Gordon said firmly.

"I don't think so either," the newspaperman agreed. "But neither of us has any proof."

"We might have — " Pete began, as he started to slide in beside Gordon. But he cut off his words as he felt Gordon's elbow jab into his ribs.

"What's that, Pete?" Lloyd Dyer prompted.

"Nothing," Pete said. He was glad the reporter didn't pursue the subject.

Soon they turned into the semicircular driveway that curved in front of the main high school building.

"Boy, we're just in time," Pete said, noticing the students beginning to pour back into the classrooms. "Lucky you gave us a ride."

114

"My pleasure," the newsman said, jockeying the coupé into a parking space. "You folks keep me posted on anything that might come up, won't you? Between us, we might be some help in breaking this case."

Real cops 'n robbers talk, Pete thought.

"We'll do what we can," Gordon said, as the coupé edged to a stop next to the curb and the young people started to pile out.

"Ouch!" Julie exclaimed, sliding off her brother's lap and bumping her head on the door frame.

But Pete hardly heard it. For, as Lloyd Dyer turned off the ignition and started to get out on the opposite side, Pete's attention was attracted by a man of medium height, in a tan hat and a gray topcoat, who suddenly had slipped around the corner of the bike shed.

"See you around, kids," Dyer said, then turned and went up the broad concrete steps and through the main entrance.

Julie hurried off toward her cooking class.

"Gordon," Pete said as soon as they were alone, " did — did you see him?"

"Yeah, yeah, I did," his tall friend answered thoughtfully. "But I don't suppose it means anything to us."

"Probably not."

"But let's have a look, anyway," Gordon said.

They approached the open-fronted bicycle shed from the rear in order not to be seen. They swung around the corner, expecting to surprise whoever was there.

The shed was empty of everything but bicycles.

"He sure disappeared in a hurry," Pete said.

"Probably someone was just checking for a stolen bike or something," Gordon rationalized. "Must have had his car parked right over there in the street. Well, guess there wasn't anything to it. Come on, we better get to class."

"Guess we're just getting jumpy, huh, Gordon?" Pete suggested.

"Could be," his friend admitted, smiling. "But that still doesn't explain why that fellow would bother to duck back out of sight as soon as we drove up."

"Maybe he didn't duck. Maybe it just looked that way to us."

"One thing is sure," Gordon said. "He wasn't around here to prune the shrubbery."

"Look, pal," Pete said, "I'm getting a stomachful of butterflies. What say we get together after school and sort of take an inventory on this whole thing? I never mind getting tackled, but I usually like to know which goal I'm headed for. Get me?"

"Yeah, I get you, Pete," Gordon said, smiling. "And I think you're right. Meet me after school. We'll dope it out."

11

Pete was unable to do much concentrating on his lessons that afternoon. There were so many other things on his mind. And, at the moment, they seemed considerably more important than conjugating verbs or studying the annual rainfall of the upper Mongolian plains.

There was also the little matter of trying to act modest while being the center of attraction to his classmates. Fellows who had never seemed to think of him as anything more than a star fullback or a whip-armed first baseman now hung on his every word. Girls who were accustomed to shouting his name from the bleachers, yet somehow managed to forget him right after the game, now gathered around as though he were a hero fresh home from battle.

There was no doubt that the power of the press was making itself felt. Having occurred in their own school laboratory and to their own science teacher, the tragic incident dominated the thoughts of all the students. Although he tried to abide by Lieutenant Coleman's warning against talking, Pete found himself feeding small, harmless morsels of information to his admiring classmates. He told just enough to whet their appetites, yet not sufficient to divulge the fact that he had had very little to do in the entire affair. Certainly his most active achievement had been to spirit the metal box out of the school building, but, above all things, that was the main one he could not mention.

It was quite apparent that Julie was receiving the same type of royal treatment from her circle of student friends. In the one glimpse Pete had caught of her between the fourth and fifth periods, she was being followed by a coterie of wide-mouthed, ogling hangers-on, boys and girls.

Yes, they were in the limelight. Despite the extreme seriousness of the entire affair, the attention was a warm breeze to Pete's ego. After all, the students had to have some pegs upon which to hang their curiosity. He and Julie served the purpose well — without actually going against their word to Lieutenant Coleman.

Pete had caught no glimpse of Gordon since they had arrived at school. He assumed that his gangling friend was receiving his own full share of fame. As a matter of fact, the morning papers had featured Gordon considerably more than they had Pete or Julie. Pete also had to admit that Gordon's quotes seemed to make more sense than did his own. Julie had remained politely silent during the previous night's activities. She had been quoted only once. Even then it had been something Gordon had said. Pete supposed that Lloyd Dyer had wanted to be charitable and give Julie some part in the whole affair.

When Pete passed the upstairs chemistry lab the door was closed, and he assumed it was locked. One reminder of last night's action was the dark stain of smoke on the door and around the edges of the casing. Another reminder that a good deal of mystery still surrounded the event was the constant presence in the

118

hallway of one of the plain-clothes men whom Pete had seen around the police station earlier that morning.

Twice during the afternoon Pete experienced considerable embarrassment. Once was when he was hurrying down the stairs and nearly ran into Hans Oberheath. The small, wizened man dropped his broom and dodged out of the way. Pete skidded to a stop on the stair landing and retrieved the broom.

"Sorry, Mr. Oberheath," he said in a raised voice as he handed him the broom. "Guess I was in too much of a hurry."

But Hans didn't seem to hear, or didn't seem to care. He looked right through Pete. Pete thought for a moment that Hans was going to say something, which in itself would have been a rare event. But, instead, the janitor simply made a grumbling sound deep in his throat, then turned and went on his way.

Pete was more concerned with avoiding Mr. Zucco. The science teacher certainly was not the kind to take lightly the painful tripping Pete had caused him that morning. Pete knew that the thanks had been no more than words meant to impress Lieutenant Coleman.

Yet, although Pete avoided going past Mr. Zucco's classroom, he failed to count on the science teacher's frequent use of the school's library and study hall. Deep in thought, Pete spotted a vacant study-hall chair and sat down — only to realize suddenly that he was seated directly across the table from the teacher.

"Oh — hello, Mr. Zucco," Pete said lamely.

Mr. Zucco's mouth began to move. His dark eyes narrowed beneath bushy brows. There were several tense seconds before any sound was forthcoming.

Then, like hot lava from an erupting volcano, the low, rumbling words burned against Pete's ears.

"You — you young smart aleck," Mr. Zucco said vehemently, yet keeping his voice low in accordance with study-hall rules. "You're going to be sorry for what you did this morning. A lot of people are going to be sorry for the trouble they're causing me."

Pete had no answer. This was not the place, and he certainly did not feel up to arguing with an intelligent man like Mr. Zucco. For, despite the man's temper, there was no denying that the science teacher was a keen-minded man, and a good, if difficult, instructor.

Furthermore his temper may not always have been such a fiery one. Students who had attended Oakmont High prior to Professor Nordland's appearance on the scene spoke of Mr. Zucco as perhaps a strict and demanding teacher, but a thorough and fair one. The big change seemed to have come over him shortly after Professor Nordland's appointment as head of the science department.

Certainly, Pete thought, whatever resentment or jealousy Mr. Zucco had would fall far short of causing the science teacher to commit murder. Yet, Pete had heard it said that an uncontrolled temper created an uncontrolled person, resulting often in disaster.

It suddenly became easy for Pete to believe — as Mr. Zucco scowled at him ominously from across the study table — that the science teacher was capable of violence. Even great violence.

Pete opened a book and stared at the page without seeing the words. He was trying to figure how to leave the study table without appearing rude. But he was saved the trouble, as Mr. Zucco slid back his own chair, rose, and strode out into the hallway.

Relieved, Pete attempted to get some studying done. But he was completely unable to concentrate on his work. He was considering going outside, in hopes that the crisp, snow-cooled air might snap his thoughts out of their confusion, but, before he had time to rise, Julie came into the study hall, spotted him, and sat down on the chair just vacated by Mr. Zucco.

" Pete," she whispered, " anything new? "

" About what? " Pete asked.

" About anything to do with poor Professor Nord-land," Julie said.

" I haven't heard anything. The lab's locked up and guarded. Hans Oberheath and Mr. Zucco are around. Can't be much new, anyway." Pete decided not to mention the man whom he and Gordon had seen duck back around the corner of the bike shed. As Gordon had said, there might have been nothing at all to it. Besides, Pete wasn't prone to take his younger sister too far into his confidences. Although he was extremely fond of her, she was still the " kid sister." Age-old tradition had it that she be treated with a certain aloofness by her older brother.

Besides, Pete figured that playing the role of detective was a man's work.

Pete wasn't sure that Gordon shared his feelings. After all, his science-minded friend had even gone so far as to ask Julie's opinion on several things. Only that morning he had solicited Julie's thoughts on a couple of issues.

Now Julie glanced around to make sure no one was

in hearing distance. " Pete," she said, " don't you think we should do something about that box? "

" Why? "

" Well, it seemed all right last night when everything was dark," his sister admitted. " But, you know, in broad daylight that doesn't strike me as such a clever hiding place."

" Let's go outside to talk. Someone may sit at this table," Pete said, leading the way to the hall.

Julie followed.

" Can't see anything wrong with the hiding place," Pete insisted. " The way I feel right now, the less I have to do with that box the better. I don't know why I didn't give it to Gordon last night, though. Keeping it was all his idea. If anyone's going to get in trouble for not turning it over to the police, he should be the fall guy."

" Pete, you know Gordon must have a mighty good reason for holding onto that box," Julie said firmly. " He would be the last person I know to keep anything from the police without a very good reason."

" Sure, sure, I know," Pete agreed. " But has it occurred to you just where we would be if that box had the name of the murderer in it, or something like that? Keeping it hidden might give the criminal plenty of time to escape halfway around the world."

" I don't think whoever did it is trying to escape halfway around the world," Julie said. " I think he's still around here someplace."

" What makes you think it's a he? " Pete asked.

" No special reason, I guess. Except I just can't imagine it being the kind of crime that a woman would

122

be assigned to do."

"What do you mean ' assigned '? " Pete asked again. "You're talking mighty crazy-like. Who assigned who — and why? "

"Well," Julie said thoughtfully, keeping her voice low and glancing around once more to be sure no one was coming, "the more I think about it, the more sense Gordon's idea makes that it all points toward some kind of undercover work."

"Real foreign spy stuff, huh? " Pete said, failing to mask his amusement. Whereas, during the freshness of the shock and the excitement of last night, he had listened attentively to Gordon's theories, time and the self-assurance that came with daylight had caused him to look with a marked disrespect upon such a dramatic and fanciful explanation. Oakmont City was just not the kind of town where such a thing could happen. Morocco, or Paris, or London, or even New York — those were the types of settings for such cloak-and-dagger activities of foreign agents. "Look, Sis," Pete went on, " don't let your imagination run away with you. Try to keep a level head."

"If anyone's not keeping a level head," Julie said sharply, " it's you. If you'd bother to read beyond the funny pages in the newspaper, you'd get an idea of what's going on in your own country. Don't think there aren't plenty of foreign agents circulating around."

"In Oakmont City? " Pete asked, amused.

"Sure, Oakmont City or anyplace else," Julie insisted. "Anyplace where something might be happening that would be of some interest and importance to them. And if Professor Nordland was doing a phase of

123

Government research, who's to say that he didn't come up with something that would be of value to some unfriendly nation? "

" You really believe that? " Pete said incredulously.

" Jeepers, Pete," Julie insisted, " it happens all the time. We even learn that in school. And why do you think we have speakers at assembly every once in a while to talk on national security? If there weren't security problems, our FBI and our Government intelligence forces probably would need to be only about half as big as they are now."

" Wow," Pete said, " who've you been talking to? "

" It's just a case of keeping your ears open in class," Julie said, " and maybe reading something besides comics once in a while."

" Lay off, Sis," Pete said, glancing around. " You're making noises like a sophomore."

Julie smiled. " I guess I am, Pete," she agreed. " But, then, you asked. Anyway, we're only guessing, but I believe pretty much the same as Gordon. I believe that Professor Nordland made a valuable discovery during his research. I believe that he sensed his life was in danger. How or why, I haven't the slightest idea. I believe he didn't mention it to Mrs. Nordland for fear her life might be in danger. If there were any clues in the tin box telling who his enemies might be, Mr. Nordland never would have asked Gordon to keep it hidden until the right person calls for it. He would have instructed him to turn it directly over to the police in case anything happened. So I think it contains whatever discovery Mr. Nordland might have made. And that it's too important even to be turned over to the local police."

"Supposing all that's correct," Pete said, "just what's the score if Professor Nordland happened to be working for some foreign Government? What if he was some kind of subversive agent himself? If you want to figure in the spy business, you've got to figure that it works both ways."

"Naturally, it's possible," Julie admitted. "But it doesn't seem likely. Especially in the face of Professor Nordland's great military and scientific service to our country since World War II."

"Well, I guess you've got something there, Sis," Pete admitted. "But I'll sure be glad when all this lousy business gets straightened out. I don't like the idea of a murderer running around here and — Say, that reminds me, what makes you think that he — if it was a he — would not have escaped halfway around the world by now? What makes you think he's still hanging around Oakmont City?"

"That's simple, Pete," Julie said. "It's quite obvious that whoever did the deed failed to get what he was after."

"Why? Maybe he got what he was after."

"He couldn't have," Julie said, and she sounded very positive. "Because the thing he wants is in that tin box. I know it just as sure as shootin'. You know it too. But you don't want to admit it."

"Yeah," Pete said, nodding, "yeah, you're right." He gulped and looked very uncomfortable. "And the whole doggone thing is right under our front porch steps!"

Just then the bell rang. Pete and Julie had to go off

in opposite directions for their last-period classes.

Pete's mind was buzzing. Julie sure had brought up some strangely provoking thoughts — some strangely frightening thoughts.

At the end of the final period Pete met Gordon in front of the school. A group of students quickly gathered around, plying them with questions. They also expounded all sorts of sinister and inane theories concerning how and why the whole tragic incident had happened.

No one even came near having a valid idea. Pete and Gordon made it a point not to be drawn into the conversations, although the temptation existed. They edged steadily down the walk, finally leaving the curiosity-consumed students far behind.

"Hey," Gordon said when they were a block away from school, "where's Julie?"

"I suppose she's gabbing with some of the girls," Pete said. "Why?"

"I doubt if she's gabbing," Gordon said defensively. "Julie doesn't waste much time just gabbing. Anyway, if we're going to discuss this business, and maybe map out some new ideas, I think all three of us should be in on it."

"Why?"

"Because the three of us have been together on it from the beginning," Gordon said, looking puzzled over Pete's apparent challenge to his sister's right of being kept informed.

" This isn't girls' stuff," Pete said stanchly. " It could be dangerous, you know." He didn't really believe it, but it sounded good. " We'd better count her out."

" I don't think . . . Whoa, there she comes now." Gordon pointed back along the sidewalk, where Julie was hurrying toward them, skipping the frozen patches of snow as she came.

" Why didn't you fellows wait? " she scolded, puffing breathlessly. " Pete, I've got some news for you. But maybe you've heard it."

" How should I know? " Pete said. " What is it? "

" Mr. Zucco is taking over Professor Nordland's chemistry classes. At least, until they can get a replacement teacher."

" Wow! " Pete exclaimed. " You . . . you mean he'll be giving the Chemistry III exams? "

" Looks like it."

" Well, that cooks me! " Pete wailed. " He'll murder me."

" Bum joke," Gordon said. " But I doubt if Mr. Zucco will bend over backward to make you look good in an exam, at that."

" He'll ruin me," Pete insisted. " He'll make me ineligible for baseball, sure as shootin'."

" Not if you know the answers to the test," Gordon said logically. " Doesn't matter what personal feelings he may have, if you get the answers right; he has to pass you."

It was slight consolation to Pete; for so much had happened during the past twenty or so hours that he didn't feel he had a single answer in his head. Over-whelmed by solemn thoughts, Pete kept wandering off the sidewalk and into snowdrifts. By the time they arrived home, snow had seeped in around the tops of his arctics so that his feet were sloshing.

"Pete, Julie," Gordon said as they turned into the Rogers' front yard, "let's go on over to my house and do a little talking."

"About what, Gordon?" Julie asked.

"Things."

"Well, it's O.K. with me," Pete said, "but I'd better go in and get some dry socks on first."

As they walked toward the porch, the footprints and general disarray of the snow at the corner of the porch steps reminded Pete of last night's activity — and of the green tin box, with all its secrets, still hidden underneath the wooden steps.

No doubt Gordon and Julie were having much the same thoughts, as they stomped the snow off their overshoes and followed him into the house.

"Hello, children," Mrs. Rogers greeted them lightly. Yet Pete thought he detected a somewhat worried expression on his mother's face. "How did everything go today?"

"All right, I guess, Mother," Julie said.

"Have you heard any new developments about last night?"

"Mom," Pete said, "we're really not supposed to talk about — "

"Pete," Gordon cut in quickly, "I don't believe in keeping secrets from your own parents. They have every right to know what we're up to."

128

"Well, Gordon," Mrs. Rogers said, smiling, "you most certainly are considerate. Peter, you might practice a little on that score."

"But nothing really new has happened, Mrs. Rogers," Gordon went on. "I don't think anyone actually believes Mr. Nordland met with an accident. But there aren't any really solid ideas about just what did take place. At least, about why it took place."

"Oh, before I forget it," Mrs. Rogers said, "Mr. Dyer, of the *Globe*, was out here to see you."

"Out here?" Pete said. "When?"

"Oh, I'd say about a half hour ago."

"But he knew we were at school," Julie said.

"Well, he mentioned that he didn't know just when school let out, and said he was coming by this way and took the chance you might be home."

"Did he say what he wanted, Mom?" Pete asked. The butterflies were beginning to gather again in his stomach. The only thing he could think of that would bring Lloyd Dyer out to the house would be to inquire about the tin box. After being with the newsman that morning — and even riding part way to school with him — Pete had figured that the tin box and the episode of getting it out of the school building had been forgotten. Now it was apparent to him that the newsman hadn't forgotten. Pete shot a startled glance at Gordon.

"No, dear," his mother was saying, "he didn't say what he wanted. Mentioned that it wasn't particularly important, though, and that he would be seeing you in the next day or so, anyway."

"Yeah," Pete said. Then: "Mom, is it O.K. if I go

129

over to Gordon's for a little while? We've got some things to talk over." He shed his wet socks, dried his feet, and pulled on a pair of fresh socks that he found hanging near the water heater on the service porch.

" Julie too, Mrs. Rogers," Gordon added quickly.

" I suppose it's all right," Pete's mother said. " Only don't be late for dinner. We'll eat around seven."

Pete knew that his mother was burning with curiosity. But she was like his father in the respect that she would offer whatever help she could, and then leave it up to Pete or Julie to make use of it. Beyond determining that Pete and Julie were not off-beam in any of their activities, the adult Rogerses subscribed to the theory of allowing their children to work out their problems in so far as they were able, and until they solicited assistance.

Pete promised himself that he would volunteer as much information as he could at the very first opportunity.

They went on outside, threaded their way through the hole in the hedge, and entered Gordon's house from the rear. After exchanging hellos with Mrs. Newhall, they went on upstairs to Gordon's room. It was located just beneath the attic at the front of the rather old-fashioned, high-roofed house.

Pete never failed to marvel at what his science-minded friend so casually called his " study." It looked much more like a movie set left over from some Frankenstein picture. There were shelves of jars containing powders and chemical solutions. There were racks of test tubes and boxes of flasks and beakers, many of which were filled with more liquids and powders.

Small boxes with sticker labels were all over. Several fiendish-looking contraptions, tied together by tangles of twisted glass tubing and short lengths of small rubber hose, occupied a large worktable. A drain hose ran out of the window from a dishpan that Gordon had converted into a sink. Another hose ran into the room from a hydrant at the side of the house near the lower front corner. This, Pete knew, was the necessary water supply for Gordon's upstairs laboratory. Only now, with the freezing winter temperature making it useless, Gordon kept his supply in a five-gallon water bottle, which, evidently, he hauled up and down the stairs as his supply demanded.

The remainder of the rather large room was occupied by books, Gordon's bed, one chair, and even a few airplane and boat models he had worked on a few years back, but had abandoned in preference to science.

Julie stood wide-eyed in the doorway.

"Heavens!" she exclaimed.

"Oh, I forgot," Gordon said, smiling, "you've never seen my study before, have you, Julie?"

"Study?" Julie said in amazement. "This is like no study I've ever imagined. Gordon, how do your folks ever allow such a conglomeration of — of —"

"My parents have nothing against my being a scientist," the tall boy said proudly. "And as long as I'm experimenting with harmless things, and using care, they don't mind."

"How do they know that you're not manufacturing Z-bombs or something up here?" Pete asked.

"My father and I often work on things together,"

Gordon said. " He knows pretty much of what's going on up here all the time."

" Well," Julie said, " I can sure see why you're an A science student. You've got almost as much stuff up here as we have at school. Everything is labeled too. I guess you know what you're doing, at that."

" Thanks," Gordon said, smiling. " I do my best not to blow our house down. Hey, Pete, you trying to figure out another of your funny gags or something? How about putting back that box of gentian violet powder, and let's get down to the business at hand."

Grinning over the memory of the fun he had had at school one day with some gentian violet, Pete returned the box of powder to the shelf. He went over and plopped down on Gordon's bed. Julie cleared some science magazines off a chair and sat down.

" I wonder what Lloyd Dyer was doing out here? " Gordon mused, by way of opening the conversation.

" You know doggone well what," Pete said. " And I don't think we're going to get away with working that shoe box gag on him. Dyer's no dummy."

" You might be right, Pete," Gordon agreed. " Although if he really gets curious, the shoe box routine is our only way out for the time being."

" There's one other way out," Pete said.

" What's that? "

" Get rid of the real box."

" You mean move it? "

" I mean get rid of it! "

" Let's not go through that again, Pete," Julie said. " Gordon has made it plain enough why we should hold onto the box a little longer, anyway."

132

"O.K., O.K.," Pete said, "so we'll hold onto it. But what do you say we get it out from under our front porch steps? It gives me the willies."

"I agree to moving it," Gordon said. "It's too damp under those steps, anyway. I don't imagine the box is very waterproof. Whatever's in it might start to mold. Besides, we may have to get it in a hurry one of these days. And it's too much in the open where it is. We'd be seen by a dozen neighbors and stuff if we ever tried moving it. Matter of fact, who's to say that Lloyd Dyer hasn't already canvassed some of the neighbors to find out if they've seen us toting such a box around?"

"I doubt it," Julie said. "It seems to me that if Mr. Dyer was at all interested about that box he would have mentioned it long ago. I don't believe he even gave it a second thought."

"Then why was he out here a while ago?" Pete reminded.

"Probably just to pick up some news," Julie said. "Let's quit making mountains out of molehills."

"Oh, I wondered what they were made of," Pete said. "I don't suppose you want to move the box, either."

"Yes, I think we should," Julie said. "Gordon, where do you suggest moving it?"

Gordon pointed to a small trap door over his head. "There's lots of room up there in the attic," he said. "It's not only good and dry, but private too. And we could get at the box any time we wanted to without being seen."

"Sounds O.K. to me," Pete agreed. "Especially since it's your attic, not ours. Let's go get it."

133

"We can't get it right now," Gordon said. "That would be like hanging out a sign advertising we have it. We've got to be careful. People will be curious about most anything we do. We'd better wait till after dark. That should be in less than an hour."

"Gordon's right," Julie confirmed.

Accepting the wait as necessary, Pete got up and started pacing back and forth. He was careful about what he touched; for he could never tell what fiendish devices Gordon might have among the tangles of chemistry equipment. He studied the labels on the bottles and cartons for a while. Then he thumbed through a few technical magazines, and generally gave the appearance of being impatient.

"What's bothering you, Pete?" Julie asked.

"Nothing in particular," her brother said, "and everything in general. The more I think about this whole thing, the more scared I get. We're all in it mighty deep, you know. Especially when it comes to that tin box. I still think we might be saving our skins if we just turn it over to the police."

"Pete," Gordon said, "we would. We definitely would — except for one thing."

"What's that?" Julie asked.

"The instructions Professor Nordland gave me were very definite in that I was to hold onto that box at all costs."

"You never said ' at all costs' before," Pete said.

"Well, I didn't want it to sound any more sinister than it actually is," Gordon explained. "And, believe me, both of you, if I didn't believe so strongly in Professor Nordland's word, I'd probably agree with you

134

that the box should be turned over to the police. As it is, I'm confident that it wouldn't do them any good in solving the case; and a great deal of harm could result if some of those papers got mislaid, or somehow were seen by the wrong eyes."

"Why can't you just tell the police that the papers are important, and that they should be locked up?" Pete wondered.

"If it were that simple," Gordon said, "I'm sure Professor Nordland would have instructed me to do it that way. Even if the police had the box, they might have to use the papers for evidence or something. And who knows how many people would have access to them, and all that? And one of those people might be just the wrong one to see the formulas or whatever the papers contain. We've got to give Professor Nordland credit for doing a lot of sensible thinking."

"You make it sound as though he was making out his last will and testament when he told you what to do and gave you the box for safekeeping," Julie said.

"I don't mean to," Gordon said. "Remember, I've had the box for several weeks. It was in my sink cabinet all the time. I believe Professor Nordland suggested that I keep it there for two reasons. One, as I've said before, no one would bother to look in a student's sink cabinet for such an important item. And, two, Professor Nordland wanted the box where he could get at it in a hurry."

"Why?"

"I think he was expecting some authorized person to come calling for it."

"You — you mean the same person you're expecting to show up and claim it?" Julie asked.

"That's about it, I guess," Gordon said. "And although it seemed to me that Professor Nordland was a little concerned and uneasy about something, I'm sure he didn't suspect there was any real danger to his life. But I think that whatever is in that box is something so important he couldn't afford to take any chances with it."

"How could he be so sure he wasn't taking a chance giving it to you?" Pete asked bluntly.

"That's a good question, Pete," Gordon said. "Only thing I can figure is that Professor Nordland was in a spot where he had to trust someone. It's pretty flattering that he chose me."

"Oh, that's natural," Pete said. "You were his top boy."

"Anyway," Gordon said, "I don't want to let him down — not if I can help it. And giving that box to anyone other than the person who properly identifies himself to receive it is taking an unnecessary chance, no matter how you figure it."

"But how will you know who is the right person?" Julie asked.

"I'll know," Gordon said with a slight smile.

"You know just how he'll identify himself?" Pete wanted to know.

"Remember, Pete," Julie reminded, "Gordon said he had a regular password or something."

"Yeah. Well, I guess it's all right," Pete said with an air of resignation. "Matter of fact, I'm glad you're doing all the figuring on this deal. I'm done in. Fagged. All I hope is that the whole thing isn't finally pinned on us. Seems to me that Lieutenant Coleman is getting

136

kind of skittish. Just like Lloyd Dyer said last night when we were first going up the stairs toward the lab, Lieutenant Coleman hasn't had a murder on his hands for a long time, and he isn't going to let anything crab his act."

" Dyer said that, huh? " Gordon mused. " He's probably part right, at that. And maybe one reason he isn't saying anything about the box is that he doesn't want us to turn it over to the police, either. He knows a scoop when he sees one. And he probably figures that he can work slowly and get it out of us a lot easier than he could out of the police. Remember that case upstate last year when Dyer was on the Midland *Courier?* "

" You mean the sabotage business with the experimental jet bomber? " Pete inquired.

" Yeah. Well, Lloyd Dyer's write-ups on that deal brought him quite a bit of fame. Even though the case was never solved, he certainly kept the entire country well informed for weeks. Big story. He's in no hurry now, I'll bet. Probably hoping it will work into something big. Say, are you sure that he mentioned — "

" Hey, Gordon," Pete interrupted suddenly, holding up a cautioning hand. He stood looking out of one of the two high dormer windows that furnished light and ventilation to the room. " Come here a minute. Quick! "

As he spoke, Pete edged to one side of the window. " Stay back out of sight," he cautioned, " but take a glance over across the street."

Gordon eased up beside him and peeked around the edge of the window casing. Across and down the street a couple of houses he saw the figure of a man standing beside the trunk of a giant elm tree. In the deepen-

ing dusk there wasn't a whole lot that could be identified about the person. But Pete had noticed something
and now Gordon did.

"The — the guy in the gray topcoat! " he exclaimed.
"Now, what do you suppose he would be doing way
out here? "

"Well, there's one thing I'm sure of," Pete said.
"He's not out here just taking a walk for his health.
What're we getting into now, Gordon? What's with this
guy? "

"I — I don't know, Pete," his friend said, and he
looked really worried. "But I know one thing. We've
got to get that box moved, and soon."

"Hey, there he goes," Pete said, pointing. "He must
have spotted us spotting him."

Julie had gone to the other dormer window and was
peering down. "I wish I could make out his face," she
said. "But it's too dark. He has his hat pulled down
pretty low too. It could be Mr. Zucco or — "

"It could be anybody," Pete cut in impatiently.
"This town is full of medium-sized guys with gray top-
coats and hats. What we need to know is who that particular one is."

But there was nothing to be done about it at the
moment. The man had walked rapidly to the corner.
Now he turned and disappeared in the direction of
town.

Remembering the incident that noon at the school's
bike shed, Pete felt uneasy. Yet he was certain of one
thing: They had not seen the last of the man in the
gray topcoat.

A FEW minutes later Julie said: "It's pretty dark. Can't we get the box now? It's about time we went home for dinner anyway."

There had been considerable silence in the room ever since the man in the gray topcoat had made his unexplained appearance and disappearance. Gordon was obviously giving it a great amount of thought, trying to puzzle it out. Pete merely gave it a little thought, then discarded it. The rapid sequence of events had him quite thoroughly confused. He decided to let Gordon and the police do the figuring.

Gordon glanced out into the gathering darkness. "I guess no one can see us," he said. "We have to be careful, though. The neighbors are certain to be somewhat curious about everything we do. Everyone likes to work on a mystery. If they see us doing anything that doesn't seem entirely normal, they might start talking. It could even reach the police, and — well, the police might not see things just our way. We can't be too careful."

"In that case," Pete said, "why don't you just go ahead and get the box? I'll keep a lookout from up here. Julie too. One person might not be noticed. Three might."

"I think we'd all better go," Gordon said. "I think we need our lookouts down there. I don't mind getting the box."

"O.K., then," Pete said, shrugging. "Let's go. We're wasting time."

"When we get downstairs," Gordon instructed, "turn left and go out through the kitchen. Then we won't disturb my folks. I hear them in the living room."

They eased downstairs, crept along the hallway to the kitchen, and went out the back door. Here they stopped on the back steps to give their eyes a chance to adjust to the darkness. It was done quickly; for the whiteness of the snow patches reflected the lights of the neighborhood and the night glow of the sky, allowing for fair visibility.

They went up the driveway until they reached the notch in the hedge, worn there by years of shuttling back and forth between houses.

"Julie," Gordon whispered, "how about you going out front and looking up and down the walk? If anyone comes in sight from either direction, whistle. Soon as we get through, we'll whistle. You'll know we've got the box."

"Mission accomplished," Pete said.

"We can meet on our back porch," Gordon went on. "Then we'll take the box up, ditch it in the attic, and that's that."

"You want me to stay here?" Pete asked hopefully.

"You'd better come with me," Gordon said. "You know just where you hid the box. Besides, you can keep a lookout too."

Julie went on down the driveway to the front walk. Gordon and Pete waited a minute for a possible whistle. None came, indicating the coast was clear.

They slipped through the hedge and started across the yard in front of Pete's house.

They had gone only a few steps in the darkness when Gordon stopped so suddenly that Pete barged right into him. Gordon was stiff as a board.

" Pete! " he gasped in a tense whisper. " Look! "

Pete leaned out so he could see past Gordon. What he saw caused a strange prickling sensation to surge along his spine.

Twenty yards ahead of them, and silhouetted against the snow, a dark figure straightened up from beside the Rogerses' porch steps. It hesitated a moment, as though seeing or sensing the boys' nearby presence.

It was much too dark to make out any more than the barest outline of the figure. But the outline was unmistakably that of a man — a man of slightly more than average height, and of medium build. He was wearing a hat and a heavy coat. Both served as excellent camouflage, although the darkness eliminated such need.

Gordon, Pete, and the man beside the porch seemed equally unable to move. Even Pete, who prided himself on the ability to act fast in an emergency, could only stand and stare into the darkness. Had he been capable of meeting the emergency represented in the strange figure a scant twenty yards away, the whole mystery might have been solved then and there. But Pete was not the first to regain his stunned senses.

With a guttural oath, the man beside the porch turned and fled. The sound of his voice snapped Pete and Gordon out of their frightened immobility. But the man quickly dodged out of sight in the darkness.

Gordon found his voice first. " Come on! " he yelled.

There was a strange tightness in his voice that Pete had never before heard.

Pete was just getting his muscles under control when Gordon made a beeline for the front steps. By the time Pete caught up to him, his friend was down on his knees in the snow, groping underneath the steps.

Pete waited numbly, staring off into the darkness, scarcely realizing that his teeth were chattering.

"How far under did you shove it, Pete?" Gordon turned his head and asked anxiously over his shoulder.

"Not far. Right there. Right where your hand is now. Can't you feel it?"

Gordon straightened up slowly and faced him. In the darkness Pete couldn't make out the expression on Gordon's face. But there was no mistaking the resignation in his friend's voice.

"It's gone, Pete," Gordon said in shocked disbelief. "The box is gone!"

"Gone? You're sure?" Pete dropped to his knees and thrust a hand in under the porch steps. He knew exactly where the box should be. The space was empty. "Come on," he cried, jumping to his feet, "let's catch that guy!"

"He's three blocks from here by now, Pete," Gordon said.

Pete realized how ridiculous his suggestion had been. Just then he heard Julie's whistle from the direction of the street.

"It's all off, Julie," Gordon called. "We're over here by your front porch."

Julie came crunching through the snow, which the night air was fast crusting over. "What's all off?" she asked.

142

"The box is gone," Pete said.

"Gone? Gone where? How?"

They told her.

"I thought I saw someone come out of the shrubbery and go running down the sidewalk," Julie said. "But it was quite a way down the block and I wasn't sure. That's why I didn't whistle sooner."

"It wouldn't have helped," Pete said. "Only way we could have caught him was to charge him right off the bat. And I — I froze stiff."

"Charge him!" Julie exclaimed. "And maybe get shot? You did just right. That tin box has been scaring the daylights out of me ever since we've had it, anyway. Frankly, I'm almost glad it's gone. Oh, I'm sorry, Gordon," she amended. "I know how important it was to you. It's important to this whole thing, I guess. But — well, it might have caused us no end of trouble before we were through."

"It might also have solved the murder of Professor Nordland," Pete said. "That's why I was against keeping it, anyway. Now — "

"No, I don't think so, Pete," Gordon corrected. "As I mentioned before, if I'd had any idea the box would have been of any use in that respect, you can be sure I would have turned it over to the police a long time ago."

"Hey, Gordon," Pete said, struck by a new idea. "You don't suppose whoever stole that box was the person you were supposed to turn it over to anyway?"

"I'm sure not," the other boy said. "I'm certain that's not the way it would be called for. Besides, the right person will simply speak the correct code name and I'll know whom to give it to."

143

"Guess it doesn't matter now," Pete said.

"I wish I knew what to do," Gordon said with ill-hidden anguish.

"I can't figure how that person knew where the box was," Pete mused.

"How about that, Gordon?" Julie asked.

"I've been wondering too," the boy said thoughtfully.

"I'm quite sure no one saw me stuff it under there last night," Pete said. "And I know I shoved it under far enough that no one could see it in the daylight."

"How do you know?" Gordon asked.

"I checked it this morning," Pete said, "just before you came over and we went down to the police station together."

Gordon didn't speak for a few minutes. Then he said, "This may sound like a crazy question, Pete, but just how did you go about checking it?"

"It sure is a crazy question," Pete said.

"You ought to be able to answer it, anyway," Julie said.

"All right. I walked around and tried to see it from every angle. Like I say, you just couldn't see anything. But just to make doubly sure, I even got down and shoved it under a little farther."

"I guess that's what did it," Gordon said.

"That's what did what?"

"You left enough tracks in the snow to lead a blind man right to it," Gordon said, yet without any particular accusation. "Walking all around it, then right to it, and kneeling down to shove it farther in out of the way. Well-l-l—"

144

"Yikes!" Julie exclaimed. "That's it. Gordon's sure right."

As though to verify the theory, the Rogerses' porch light suddenly flared on, bathing the snow around them in its yellowish light. There were various tracks in the snow around the front yard. But by far the majority of them were in a close radius around the right side of the porch — particularly around the edge of the steps.

The front door opened and Mrs. Rogers stood silhouetted in the doorway. "Are you children out there?" she called, peering into the darkness.

"We're right here, Mom," Pete answered.

"I thought I heard talking," Mrs. Rogers said. "Well, you'd better come in now. Dinner's just about ready."

"We'll be right in, Mother," Julie said.

Mrs. Rogers went back inside and closed the door, but left the porch light on.

"Well," Pete said, "I guess I kind of fouled things up after all, Gordon. I should have known better than to make all those tracks. Guess I'm about due for a brain overhaul."

"No point in crying over spilled milk, Pete," Gordon consoled. "I doubt that any of us would have thought of it at the time. We've had plenty on our minds. Our only job now is to figure out who it was that saw the tracks and got the box."

"He'd be the murderer too, wouldn't he, Gordon?" Julie asked.

"Probably."

"Maybe we should figure out who knows we had the

145

box to begin with," Pete suggested.

" I doubt if that would solve anything," Gordon said. " Whoever is behind this thing no doubt has investigated every possibility. No matter who it was, he must have known there would be some kind of container involved. Had to be something in which to keep the papers."

" In that case it could have been just a little envelope," Pete said.

" Not too little," Gordon said. " The way in which Professor Nordland's office was looted indicated that the person was looking for more than just individual papers. He didn't even bother to thumb through the various stacks of papers in the drawers. He seemed to be hunting for some kind of package that would have everything together."

" How do you know that? " Pete wondered.

" Well, that's the way Lieutenant Coleman explained it to me when we were in the lab together," Gordon said. " Only the lieutenant figures that the murderer got what he was after."

" And supposing we know better," Pete said. " What makes you think anyone would suspect that we had the box, and come snooping around here? "

" You're not forgetting the guy in the gray topcoat, are you, Pete? What made him come snooping around? I'm sure that getting hold of whatever is in that box has been carefully planned for some time. I believe the plan went haywire when Professor Nordland discovered and recognized whoever was ransacking his office."

" You must be right," Pete said, " I — I can't argue."

" Fact is," Gordon went on, " as far as the tin box goes, most anyone could have come driving or wandering past here today and figured out where the box was hidden. That is, anybody who might suspect that we had it in the first place."

" But who would suspect us, Gordon? " Julie asked.

" Whoever was after that stuff didn't figure to leave any stone unturned," Gordon said. " The way we've been right in the middle of things ever since the explosion last night makes us prime suspects."

" Your being such a favorite of Professor Nordland's might have something to do with it too," Pete added.

" Pete, we'd better get in," Julie reminded. " Mother doesn't like having to call us more than once."

" Right," Pete said, then searched Gordon's face in the glow from the porch light. " Just one more question, pal? "

" Go ahead, Pete."

" What now? "

" I — I'm not sure," Gordon said thoughtfully. " It's a real pickle."

" It has been a pickle ever since we saw the first flash of that explosion last night," Pete said. " Someone's got to unpickle it, and mighty quick too. I've had about all I can take. Having that box swiped out from under us could cook our goose, but good."

" Pete's right, Gordon," Julie confirmed her own feelings. " If anything, we're getting farther away from a solution. In fact, it's very doubtful that we are being any help either to Professor Nordland, Mrs. Nordland, or to the police. As Pete says, having that box stolen just about fixes us."

" I'll admit it didn't help any," Gordon said.

" So, I repeat," Pete prompted, " what now? "

" I'll figure out something tonight," Gordon said. " Don't you two worry. I'll have something worked out by morning."

THE following morning, Saturday, Gordon proved that he wasn't the type of fellow to moon over a bad break. He knocked at the Rogerses' back door just as Pete came out of his room for breakfast. Julie was already at the table spooning partly frozen strawberries onto her cereal.

" Come in, Gordon," Mrs. Rogers invited.

Gordon stomped the snow off his arctics and entered. " Bro-ther," he said, " it's real nippy outside this morning."

" Yeah, I bet," Pete said. " Look at the length of those icicles hanging from the eaves. Good morning to stay in bed."

" Not this morning," Gordon said. " We've got things to do."

" Well, before you start doing them, Gordon," Mrs. Rogers suggested, " won't you sit down and have a bowl of cereal with Julie and Pete? "

" Thanks, Mrs. Rogers, but I just ate breakfast."

" But a growing boy like you can always eat an extra bowl of cereal, Gordon," Mr. Rogers put in, coming into the kitchen and picking up the conversation.

148

" Especially with strawberries."

" Oh, strawberries," Gordon said.

" Change your mind? " Mrs. Rogers asked.

" Guess you twisted my arm," Gordon said, smiling.

" Now," Pete said, after his friend from next door had brought a chair in from the dining room and sat down at the table, " just what were you saying about our having things to do? "

Gordon paused in ladling some strawberries onto his cereal. He looked around the table at Pete and Julie and Mr. Rogers. He glanced at Pete's mother, who had gone to the pantry to fill the sugar bowl. He seemed to be trying to decide something. Then he relaxed and leaned back.

" I guess there's not much point in trying to be secretive about it," he said.

" No point at all, if you're worried about my folks," Pete said.

" Well, I didn't mean it just that way, Pete," Gordon defended.

" Look, kids," Mr. Rogers cut in, " don't let this thing become awkward just because Mother and I are here. It can wait until you get outside. Or maybe we older folks could leave the room." He smiled, but Pete didn't miss overtones of disappointment and impatience in his father's words.

" I think it's time that we spilled the whole story to our parents, Gordon," Pete prompted.

" You mean there's more than we've been reading in the papers? " Pete's father asked.

" The tin box," Julie said.

" And what tin box is that? "

For the next ten minutes Mr. and Mrs. Rogers listened to the three young people pour out the entire story in a sort of verbal relay. Much of it didn't seem to be news to Mr. Rogers. The realization came to Pete that his father had not been as disinterested in the affair as he might have appeared outwardly. It occurred to Pete that his father probably had been out doing some inquiring of his own.

"It should come as no great surprise to you, Pete," Mr. Rogers said, seeming to read his thoughts, "that both your mother and I are somewhat concerned with what our children are up to. And when there seems to be some connection with murder — near or remote — well, sure, I've been doing some leg work, asking some questions and getting some answers."

"Father," Julie said, absently stirring her cereal with her spoon, "we — we haven't been fair, have we?"

"On the contrary," Mr. Rogers said. "You've been very fair. You made a promise to Lieutenant Coleman not to say any more than you had to — even to your parents. You kept your promise. Anyway, I'm afraid I should have been of no particular help had you told me. Detective work is a little out of my line. You did right. If I hadn't thought so, I'd have put the pressure on you night before last, when you came home carrying the worries of the world on your faces. Mother and I aren't blind, you know."

"We certainly knew something was up," Mrs. Rogers verified. "But you children are grown-up enough to have some judgment. We decided to let you exercise it freely — at least for a while."

"I must say that the tin box routine is pretty baffling," Mr. Rogers said. "And I'm not so sure that you acted wisely in not turning it over to the police right away. In fact, I'm trying not to talk like an attorney. If I did, I'm afraid you would practically hear the jail doors slamming behind you."

"I — I know, Mr. Rogers," Gordon said in defense, " but I had promised Professor Nordland that I'd keep it until the proper person identified himself to receive it."

"Personal promises take no precedence over the law," Mr. Rogers said. "But there I go, talking like a lawyer. Anyway, I can understand your point of view. Your loyalty left little choice of action. The awkward part about your keeping your promise to Professor Nordland is that you no longer have the tin box. It's not going to be any less awkward when you tell Lieutenant Coleman about the box. It may even complicate things a great deal in getting to the bottom of this case."

"I think we should tell him now, don't you, Mr. Rogers?" Gordon asked. "We — we can't get in much deeper than we are now."

"By all means you should tell Lieutenant Coleman," Mr. Rogers said. "There's nothing to hide now, promises or no promises. From here on out it appears to me that it's going to take the combined thinking and efforts of everyone to get this very serious business solved. If you want me to go down with you, I'll do what little I can to help soften the blow. For I don't imagine the lieutenant is going to be overjoyed when he learns you've been holding out on him."

"I — I sure appreciate your offer, Mr. Rogers," Gordon said, " but — well, I got into this myself. It seems

151

it's kind of my duty to face the music and get out of it myself. Of course, I can't speak for Julie and Pete. Actually, I think if I'd listened a little more to them, things might not be as fouled up as they are now."

"That's boloney," Pete scoffed. "Maybe we argued a little once in a while, but no one was forcing us to stick with you and your ideas. We're in it just as deep as you are. And we'll take our medicine right along with you. Huh, Julie?"

Julie managed to smile. It seemed that the only time her bigger brother was willing to count her in on something was when that something was trouble. "Sure," she said, "I wouldn't miss it for the world."

Soon Pete and Julie bundled themselves up against the cold, and the three of them started toward town. There were long minutes of silence as they crunched across the occasional patches of crusted snow on the sidewalk. Each of them seemed to be quietly fortifying himself against whatever wrath their new testimony would bring down upon them.

"If it's all right with you two," Gordon said finally, "I'd just as soon do most of the talking."

"The pleasure is all yours," Pete said willingly. "And I have the feeling that you'd better be in your best golden voice when you do it."

"There doesn't seem to be any activity at Mrs. Nordland's house," Gordon commented as they walked past. "She's sure nice. I hope this business gets cleared up so that there's no suspicion on her, or on the kind of work Professor Nordland was doing."

"That goes for me too," Pete said, "for our sake as well as hers. We'll really be up to our necks in trouble if it turns out that Professor Nordland was on someone else's team."

Gordon didn't bother to answer, since he obviously thought the statement ridiculous to begin with.

By the time they reached the civic center, the sun was driving the chill from the air. Pete unzipped his Windbreaker, and Julie brushed the hood of her snow jacket back from her head.

"Guess it's too early for any reporters to be around," Pete commented, noting the vacant front steps to the police station.

"They might be inside," Gordon said. "Incidentally, before we go to see Lieutenant Coleman, I want to check something with Sergeant Haskins, if he's in."

"Where does he figure in this business?" Pete wanted to know.

"Well, something you said last night kept coming back to my mind," Gordon explained. "That, and something that Sergeant Haskins said when he was driving us toward school yesterday."

"What's that?"

"Well, it's hardly worth mentioning," Gordon said offhand, but not so offhand that Pete didn't realize it would be worthless trying to pump him for further information at the moment.

The sergeant was at his desk, which was located to the right and just inside of the main entrance to the police station. "Hi, kids," he greeted, as the three of them walked up to him.

"Good morning, sir."

"Sergeant Haskins," Gordon said, getting right down to business, "you remember the other night

153

when Pete called in about the explosion at school? "

"Pretty early in the morning for foolish questions, isn't it?" the sergeant said, scowling. "Of course I remember it. Why?"

"Well, yesterday when you were driving us toward school you mentioned that you had the habit of jotting down things on a pad as they came in over the phone."

"That's right," the policeman admitted. "My memory's not too good, so I don't take any chances. I scribble the messages down as they come in. So?"

"You — you wouldn't happen to have the paper that you scribbled Pete's call on the other night, would you?" Gordon tried to sound casual, but Pete sensed the tension behind each word.

"Wouldn't be surprised," Sergeant Haskins said. "I usually toss 'em in this file basket after I've made out my regular report. Just a kind of double check, you know. Don't usually throw them away until a week or so later."

"I — I wonder," Gordon said, "could we see it?"

"The report?"

"No, the piece of paper you jotted the message on."

Sergeant Haskins shrugged and began riffling through the papers in the wire basket that sat on the right-hand corner of his desk. "Well, now," he said, "maybe I did toss that one away. But I sure thought — oh, here it is!" He brought out a sheet of yellow paper torn off a scratch pad which still occupied a part of his desk top. He handed it to Gordon. "Don't know whether you can read it or not."

Gordon stared at the paper silently, while Pete and Julie cast puzzled glances at each other.

154

"Oh, I can read it all right," Gordon said thoughtfully. "I can read every word. Sergeant Haskins, do you still need this?"

"Not any more," the policeman said. "Why? You want it?"

"Yes, if I may."

"Souvenir hunter, huh?" Sergeant Haskins said, laughing. "Give you the whole scratch pad if you want."

"Thanks," Gordon said, "but this one piece will do. Is Lieutenant Coleman in?"

"He's in."

"Wonder if we could talk to him?"

"Well, let's see." Sergeant Haskins pressed one of the buttons on the boxed intercom.

"Yes, Sergeant?" Lieutenant Coleman's voice came out of the box.

"The kids are out here, Lieutenant," Sergeant Haskins said. "Want to know if they can talk to you."

"Count me in on that too."

The three young people turned to see Lloyd Dyer coming across the room toward them.

"Who was that last voice?" Lieutenant Coleman asked.

"The *Globe* just arrived," Sergeant Haskins explained.

"Dyer?"

"Yes."

"Oh, well, let the kids come in. I'll talk to Dyer later."

"Lieutenant Coleman," Gordon said, putting his head down near the intercom, "if it's all right with you, it's all right with us for Mr. Dyer to hear what we've got to say. It — it'll save having to go over it again later."

"O.K., O.K.," Lieutenant Coleman's words carried a shrug. "All of you come on in. Got any friends, bring 'em too. This is just a police station." The intercom snapped off.

It was obvious to Pete that Lieutenant Coleman wasn't in the best of moods that morning. He questioned the advisability of Gordon's plan at the moment.

"Thanks, pal," Lloyd Dyer said to Gordon. "Where were you folks yesterday afternoon? I was out to your place to see you. Say, have you got some hot news? The boss has been riding me for some kind of new angle on this business. Ever since yesterday noon things seem to be getting more stalemated. No murderer, no real motive — just guesses, and — Well, you know something? This whole thing might wind up to be an accident, after all."

"I don't think so," Gordon said, starting toward the door with Lieutenant Coleman's name on it.

"Hello, folks," the detective said, glancing up. "I don't want to seem rude, but I've got a lot of things and thinking to do this morning. So let's have it on the line as quickly as possible."

"Yes, sir," Pete said, nudging Gordon to get started.

"Gordon wants to tell you about the tin box," Julie said.

"Tin box?" Lieutenant Coleman said, with only moderate interest. "I really don't have time for riddles, and —"

Gordon started talking then. He began back on the

156

night of the explosion. He explained in detail the moment when Pete was downstairs telephoning, and Julie was in the hallway fighting nausea brought on by the delayed impact of realizing what had happened to Professor Nordland. It had been the moment that Gordon considered his best opportunity to remove the tin box from his sink cabinet and spirit it downstairs to his book locker. He thought he had managed even to get it past Julie without her noticing it. Her back had been turned toward him as she leaned weakly against the wall in the hallway. But even in the very dim light, Julie explained, she had caught a glimpse of the box. Yet she hadn't been particularly concerned at the moment.

Gordon went on to tell about the incident in the darkened downstairs hallway, when Pete, mistaking him for some sort of foe, launched the tackle which tangled them both up against the water fountain, sending the box clanking down the hallway.

Leaving the action at that point, Gordon backtracked to the day a couple of weeks ago when Professor Nordland had called him into his small cubicle of an office and had entrusted him with the box. As best he could, Gordon explained what he thought were the reasons for the science teacher's giving him the box. He made it clear that they were only guesses; for Professor Nordland had seemed to depend more upon his friendship and trust for Gordon than upon furnishing details. Gordon had returned the trust by not asking questions. To him it had seemed a very simple matter of friend helping friend. He admitted to Lieutenant Coleman that he had suspected everything was not just

157

right with Professor Nordland at the time. But he had trusted the science teacher, and knew that if Professor Nordland had wanted him to know the various reasons for his actions he would have explained them without being asked.

While Gordon talked calmly, as though his mind were miles away, Pete kept glancing at Lieutenant Coleman. The detective sat stiffly, disciplining himself to silence. He seemed to realize that Gordon was oblivious to everything else except the complete telling of the story. As a policeman, Lieutenant Coleman knew that the first uninterrupted telling was the most important, and usually the most accurate.

But Pete could see the white knuckles on the detective's tightly clenched fist. He could see the muscles, bowstring-taut, stretched across the lieutenant's cheekbones. Pete could only guess that Lieutenant Coleman was striving mightily to restrain himself — striving to give Gordon full opportunity to tell his story. What would happen once Gordon had finished, Pete dared not even guess.

After telling all he knew about Professor Nordland's entrusting the tin box to him, Gordon went forward again and picked up the story where the police, including Lieutenant Coleman, had arrived at the school in answer to Pete's telephone call. He skipped quickly over the visit to the upstairs lab with Lieutenant Coleman, Lloyd Dyer, and the others.

He told in detail about how he and Pete and Julie had managed to spirit the box out of the school building — even under the eyes of the patrolmen, who were too busy with Hans Oberheath to notice. He told of

158

their anxiety over Lloyd Dyer's having seen Pete and Julie with the box. Then of how relieved they were that the newsman apparently had made no connection of the box with the incident in the chemistry lab.

Recalling the incident, Lloyd Dyer laughed softly and shook his head, as though to say, " Well, I'll be doggoned! " But he didn't say anything; for, like Lieutenant Coleman, he was making a conscious effort not to interrupt Gordon's tale.

Gordon explained how Pete had hidden the box under the front steps at the Rogerses' house. He complimented Pete by saying that he thought it had been a brain storm to hide it there. For, undoubtedly, it would be the least likely place that anyone might look.

Gordon took the blame upon himself for not thinking of the tracks in the snow, and how they might serve to give away the location of the box.

After telling about seeing the fellow in the gray topcoat hanging around the neighborhood, Gordon finished off his story by announcing simply how the box had been stolen practically out of their hands.

He was very sorry for the whole thing. But, after all, he had been carrying out a promise to Professor Nordland, and if things had not suddenly gone wrong —

It was difficult for Pete to determine whether Lieutenant Coleman sensed that the story was finished, or whether he simply was no longer able to control himself.

" This takes the rag off the bush! " he bellowed, smashing his fist down upon the desk top so hard that the pen jumped right out of the ink stand. " You three kids may not know it, but I could throw the book at you. Concealing evidence, obstructing justice, failing to report . . . Do you know what I could do — just short of hanging? "

Lieutenant Coleman was mad, and Pete had the impression that the detective could back up everything he had said. The impact of the thought brought him no pleasure. No one said a word, while Lieutenant Coleman vented the fury that had been building up in him ever since Gordon first started talking.

" And now the box is gone," the detective's voice began to taper down to a more normal tone, " and you have the gall to stand there and treat this as though it's not important — as though it's just one of those things that happens to everybody twice a week or so."

" No, sir," Gordon spoke up finally, " we don't think it's at all unimportant, Lieutenant Coleman. It's very, very important. But I don't believe it would have anything to do with catching Professor Nordland's murderer."

" You don't believe! " the detective said bitingly. " Well, let me tell you this — " he looked hard from Gordon to Pete and to Julie, " each of you is implicated in this. Up to your necks. No matter how much Newhall here wants to grab off the blame, you other two knew everything that was going on, and were in on it just as deeply as he was. Any one of you could have called a halt any time and come down here to lay the whole business on the line. Right? "

Pete gulped and nodded.

Julie said: " Gordon had made a promise to Professor Nordland. He trusted him. A promise is a pretty important thing and — "

"Promise!" Lieutenant Coleman bellowed. "Young lady, just in case you've forgotten, there's a murderer loose!"

THE discussion in Lieutenant Coleman's office continued for another ten or fifteen minutes. No one came forth with any particularly valid theory concerning who might have taken the box from beneath the porch steps.

"I don't eliminate anyone who has been in on this case," the detective said. "We haven't had enough evidence to hold anyone out of circulation. It might be Oberheath, Zucco, the guy in the gray topcoat, Dyer here, myself — this office doesn't count anyone out on these things. It might also have been a complete stranger whom we know nothing about. So what we're doing is looking for that proverbial needle in the haystack."

"We've sure wondered about that fellow in the gray topcoat," Pete said.

"We've known he's around," Lieutenant Coleman said. "But he hasn't done anything particularly suspicious — at least, up to now."

"Shouldn't you bring him in for questioning?" Gordon said.

"Sure, but bringing him in might mean that we'd never see the box again. Or what's in it. I think it's better if we just put a tail on him. Watch what he's doing. If he's the one, he'll probably lead us right to the box.

Chances are that the theft and the murder are the work of one person."

" But what if he escapes? " Julie asked.

" That's right," Pete said. " If he's the one who got the box, he's probably a thousand miles from here already."

" You kids don't give the Oakmont City police the credit they deserve, I'm afraid," Lieutenant Coleman said. " There are only three roads leading out of town, as you know. We've had a check on each one of them ever since night before last — within a half hour of the killing. Without too much fuss and muss, we know exactly who's coming in and who's going out of Oakmont City, and, in most cases, why."

" Regular roadblocks," Pete said dramatically.

" Not roadblocks as you probably think of them," Lieutenant Coleman corrected. " Just good, simple, thorough police work. And we pay particular attention to strangers. So you can be sure that the guy in the gray coat is still around here. He'll have a tail on him within the next half hour." The chief detective flipped a switch and gave his brief instructions over the office intercom.

" What the lieutenant is making clear," Lloyd Dyer offered, rising to leave, " is that the police have not been loafing on this case."

" Well, I'm sure of that," Gordon said.

" But the box is gone," Julie said simply. " And no one knows where it is, or — "

" Young lady," Lieutenant Coleman interrupted quickly, as his neck started to turn red above the collar of his suit, " if we had known about the box, it wouldn't be gone. And besides that — "

" Gentlemen," Lloyd Dyer cut in, obviously wanting to prevent a renewal of the detective's earlier wrath, " I'm going to have to leave. I think I have enough information to bring the public up to date. That missing-box business will make a lulu of a yarn. I have a couple other stories to cover; so, if you'll excuse me, I'll see you later on."

" Dyer," Lieutenant Coleman said, " I don't care if you mention the box in your write-up. But don't mention about our police checks on the traffic in and out of Oakmont City. No point in disturbing the public — or tipping off the criminal."

" Right," Lloyd Dyer acknowledged the detective's request. " Not a word." He turned and left the office.

" Well, kids," Lieutenant Coleman said in a more kindly tone than he had used since the subject of the missing box was first brought up, "I don't suppose you have any other simple little items to mention? " He even awarded them a slight smile. " So we might as well call it a day. Keep in touch."

" Yes, sir," Gordon said, rising. " And — and Lieutenant Coleman? "

" Yes? "

" I'm sorry."

" You were doing what you thought was right," the detective said tolerantly. " Only next time you get into any kind of situation where police work might be involved, you go to the police first. In the meantime, we still have this mess to figure out."

" We'll solve it, sir," Gordon said impetuously.

" That's right," Lieutenant Coleman said absently,

as he turned to talk to a patrolman who had just come in the door. " But you kids keep out of the way."

Gordon, Julie, and Pete left the police station and started automatically toward home.

" Boy, we've had it, huh, Gordon? " Pete said. " The lieutenant wasn't exactly sparing the horses."

Gordon smiled. " Thanks for standing up with me," he said. " You didn't need to. I'm afraid I was the one who dug most of the hole we're in now. I don't see any reason why you two have to be stuck in it too."

" I don't either," Pete said. " Guess the only thing that's keeping me in is that I'm not in the habit of running out when the game goes a little against me."

" If this is a game," Julie said, " I'll stick to knitting."

" Well, you know what I mean."

" Sure, I know," Julie said. " And I'm not running out either, Gordon. Not that I'm exactly delighted with the whole affair, but — Well, I don't like abandoning sinking ships either."

" So all three of us are still stuck," Pete said. " What comes next? "

" Maybe it hasn't occurred to either of you," Julie reminded, " but do you know that we could simply keep out of this whole business, and let the police handle it? They get paid for it. We just seem to get into trouble. After all, Gordon, you tried your best to keep your promise to Professor Nordland. That didn't seem to work out. Lieutenant Coleman just got through telling us to keep out of the way. If we do anything else he doesn't approve of — well, I'm afraid — "

" We'll be very careful not to get in the way," Gordon agreed. " But I have a couple ideas that I want to work on."

"Ouch!" Pete exclaimed. "Here we go again!"

"I repeat," Gordon said, "you can pull out of this any time. I won't blame you if you do. In fact —"

"Look, pal," Pete cut in, "I call my own plays. When I want to forfeit the game, I'll do the deciding. We're this far and still out of jail. And one thing you can say, it hasn't been a dull life."

When they arrived in front of the Rogerses' house, Julie said: "I have to go in and help Mother for a while. I don't suppose you fellows need me."

"Want me to answer that, Sis?" Pete said.

"Never mind." Julie turned into the driveway, leaving the two boys together on the front walk.

"What are you planning to do now, Gordon?" Pete asked. "I'm not too anxious to go in my house. Dad's home today, and he may be figuring out some jobs for me to do. Usually he never thinks of them unless I'm right handy. Then something reminds him, and — pow — I'm loaded with work."

Pete didn't mention it, but Gordon had had a strange look in his eyes ever since their arrival at the police station that morning. Pete wanted to know more about what that look meant. He also knew he would have to find out without too much prying, or not at all.

Gordon said: "Well, I'm not going to do anything special, I guess. Come on over if you want. But you're likely to catch it if your dad thinks you're ditching out on your chores."

"Who's ditching? He'll know where I am. Julie can tell him. He can call across the hedge if he needs me. Come on."

They went in the back way and up to Gordon's room. Pete flopped down on his friend's bed and began thumbing through some magazines. He wasn't particularly interested in the contents. He was more interested in Gordon. Gordon began to wander rather aimlessly around the room. Pete knew the signs. His friend was deep in thought.

He stopped to tinker with one of the weird combinations of beakers, flasks, and twisted glass tubing. Then he moved on to other scientific gadgets he had constructed there in his upstairs room. It was rather obvious to Pete that Gordon was not particularly interested in what he was doing. He guessed that his friend kept moving around in order to discourage any questions that Pete might want to ask.

Then, when Gordon arrived at the section of shelves that held his rather large array of chemicals, his interest in what he was doing seemed to grow more keen. Pete knew that many of the chemicals were leftovers from various chemistry sets that Gordon's parents had bought him from time to time. Then too, Gordon made a regular habit of budgeting part of his allowance and neighborhood lawnmowing earnings for science supplies. These he ordinarily purchased at either the Oakmont Super Drugs or at a large hobby shop in the middle of town.

Pete watched him studying the labels on various small bottles and small cardboard containers. There was one small carton that Gordon seemed particularly interested in. But his back was to Pete, who was unable to tell which one it was. Actually, he wasn't overly interested anyway.

" Well," Pete said after a while, getting up to stretch, " I guess there's not a whole lot to do over here, at that.

166

Suppose I might as well go on home and take the chance of Dad's thinking of any work that needs doing."

Gordon turned around, seeming to make an obvious effort to pull himself out of his thoughts. " Sorry, Pete," he said. " Guess I'm not much fun to be with."

" Oh, I'm not complaining, pal," Pete said. " But you sure are all wound up in something, aren't you? "

" Yeah. Kind of."

" Got anything to do with this morning? "

" Sure."

" No point in my asking what it is, I suppose," Pete said. " If you wanted me to know, you wouldn't have been giving me the silent treatment during the past ten minutes. Right? "

Gordon walked over and sat in the chair next to his bed. " Pete," he said, " I've just got a hunch."

" Hunches are a dime a dozen, pal," Pete scoffed.

" Well, it's really more than a hunch. Nothing positive, but more than a hunch."

" All right," Pete said impatiently, " I'm in this thing too, you know. Tell me about it. What were you trying to cover up with all that wandering around and reading bottle labels you've been doing? "

" I wasn't covering up, Pete," Gordon said. " Oh, maybe a little bit. I was trying to get an idea to jell."

" Any success? "

" I — I think so, Pete. I think we might build a trap for catching our man."

Pete said, " Maybe if you told me about it I could come up with an idea or two that might help."

" Pete," Gordon said, " I know you're going to get

sore, but — well, I can't tell you about it. Not just yet."

"Oh, great!" Pete said. "I'm only in this thing up to my ears, and you still want to carry on a one-man campaign."

"We just can't take any chances, Pete," Gordon explained. "The less people know about it, the more chance there will be of its working. Any little hint, even someone's glance at the wrong time, might tip the whole thing off — and ruin our big chance of catching our man."

Pete shrugged. In the first place, he figured that his friend was probably overdoing the mystery bit. In the second place, the morning's session in Lieutenant Coleman's office had left his mind pretty limp. "O.K.," he said, "so don't tell me. I don't believe I really care, anyway. I've got a pretty good idea, despite Lieutenant Coleman's roadblocks, that whoever's behind this whole rotten business beat it far, far away from Oakmont City right after he got hold of the tin box."

"I can't agree, Pete," Gordon said.

"That's your privilege, pal," Pete said, turning toward the door. "But as long as you don't have any more reason for your thinking than I do for mine, let's just call it a draw."

"Oh, but I have a reason," Gordon said. "Might be nuts, but it's a reason just the same."

"But it's not for my lily-white ears to hear," Pete guessed. "Is that it?"

"Not exactly," Gordon said.

"It wouldn't be that you know where the tin box is, would it?" Pete asked, eying his friend suspiciously.

"Hardly," Gordon said. "But I sure wish I did. And

168

that's why we have to be so very careful."

"Careful about what?"

"About tipping off the guy who has it," Gordon explained. "If he knows anyone's suspicious, he might get rid of it, Professor Nordland's papers and all. That would ruin everything, wouldn't it?"

"I don't know," Pete said, shrugging. "This whole thing is way beyond me. What you're forgetting is that we don't know who we might be tipping off to what — or why."

"That's where you're wrong, Pete," Gordon said. "Well, maybe I don't know exactly, but I have a pretty good hunch."

"So-o?" Pete said lazily. "About what?"

"About who did it."

"I think you really mean it," Pete said.

"I do mean it, Pete," Gordon insisted. "Of course, like I say, it's just a hunch. But I think we can prove it — one way or another."

CHAPTER

16

PETE began to have that feeling again of moving around in a nightmare. Gordon's idea seemed to have taken shape. He refused to listen to Pete's sudden arguments against going right back down to the police station.

"Why don't you think about it a while longer?" Pete suggested. "Whatever it is, it might not make so much sense if you kick it around a little more. We can't afford to go off the deep end with Lieutenant Coleman any more."

"I've thought about it plenty," Gordon said. "And if there's a murderer around here, we can't just wait and let him keep running loose."

"If?" Pete challenged. "I thought you said you knew who it is."

"I didn't say positively," Gordon reminded. "If I knew for sure, all I'd do would be call Lieutenant Coleman."

"So we're going on a wild-goose chase," Pete scoffed. "Gordon, aren't we in enough hot water now? Do we have to — "

"Pete," his friend said sharply, "it's no wild-goose chase. Now, look, if you want to stay home, that's perfectly O.K."

"Don't try to brush me off," Pete said firmly.

"Then let's go."

"Back to the police station?"

"Sure."

Pete shrugged.

Gordon insisted that they stop by for Julie. "She has a right to know what's going on," he said.

Julie was puzzled that they would be going back down to the police station, but she reserved her questions and got her coat.

"Come to think of it," Gordon said, as they were ready to leave the Rogers house, "it might be a good idea to get Mr. Dyer."

"Yeah, he's pretty sharp," Pete said. "Good guy to have on your team. He sure stepped in and helped keep Lieutenant Coleman off our necks a couple of times this morning. And I've got a feeling that what-ever you're up to — well, that we'll probably need all the help we can get."

"I guess I'm thinking more about the story in to-morrow's *Globe*," Gordon said. "I didn't like the hints in this morning's paper that Professor Nordland's re-search might not have been on the up and up. If we can prove that it was, I'd like to have Lloyd Dyer right on the spot to write the correction. How do you sup-pose Mrs. Nordland must feel?"

"It would certainly be awful for her," Julie said, "if anything was proved against Professor Nordland's character — or patriotism. She's such a nice person."

"So was Professor Nordland," Gordon said fervently.

Lloyd Dyer was not at the *Globe* office, but was ex-pected back momentarily. Gordon left a message ask-ing him to meet them at the Oakmont City police sta-tion as soon as it was convenient.

The midafternoon sun was dropping toward the rim of the western foothills just outside Oakmont City as the young people arrived at the civic center.

"Going to be a cold one tonight," Julie commented, shivering.

"Cold enough for me already," Gordon said.

Sergeant Haskins looked up from a magazine he was reading as they entered. "Well, you kids didn't get enough this morning, huh?" he said, smiling.

"Something new developed," Gordon explained. "Wonder if we could see Lieutenant Coleman?"

"He's busy right now," the sergeant said. "You sure you want to see him? He's not in too good a mood — not for pranks."

171

" We don't prank," Pete said.

Gordon gave him a glance of approval.

" Have a seat, then," the sergeant said. " Soon's he's finished with Dyer, maybe he'll see you."

" Lloyd Dyer? " Gordon asked.

" Are there other Dyers around here? "

" Well, we wanted to see Mr. Dyer too," Gordon said. " In fact, we stopped in at the *Globe* office. They weren't sure where he was, and — "

Just then the door to Lieutenant Coleman's office opened. Lloyd Dyer said a few parting words, then turned and saw the young people standing near Sergeant Haskins' desk.

" Well, speak of the devil," he said. " The lieutenant and I were just talking about you."

" Oh-h? " Gordon said.

" Yeah. We were trying to unscramble some of the theories you've been coming up with every once in a while," the news reporter said. " Someplace along the line something should begin to make a bit of sense. You sure you've been giving out with everything you know? "

" What do you mean? " Gordon said.

" A trio who will hold out on that tin box business as long as you did — well, you can't blame anyone for being suspicious that you might be holding out on something else. Know what I mean? " Lloyd Dyer smiled.

He was still standing just outside the open doorway into Lieutenant Coleman's office. " Hey, who's out there? " the detective called.

" It's the kids," Lloyd Dyer explained over his shoulder.

"Oh, no, not those kids again!" A chair scraped back, and Lieutenant Coleman appeared in the doorway beside the newsman. "What now?"

"Mr. — Mr. Dyer guessed it, I'm afraid," Gordon managed.

"Guessed what?"

"We — I've been holding back something," the tall boy confessed.

For a moment it was touch and go between Lieutenant Coleman and his temper. Then, with a voice under the obvious strain of control, he said: "Come on in here to the true confession department. All of you. You'd better get this too, Dyer."

The three young people and Lloyd Dyer went inside the detective's office. Lieutenant Coleman closed the door. When they were seated, he said, "This had better be good." He leaned back to listen, then added, "If by any chance you still have that box — well, I'm not making any promises about what will happen to you, or —"

"We don't have it," Gordon said quickly.

"I can back that up," Pete said.

"Matter of fact," Gordon went on, "maybe it's just as well it was stolen. It should furnish the necessary clue to catch the thief — and murderer."

Pete sucked in his breath. Gordon was going a bit overboard, he thought.

"Go on," Lieutenant Coleman prompted.

"I — I didn't even tell Pete or Julie about it," Gordon went on, "but that first night when Pete hid it under the front steps of his house, I got to worrying about that box falling into improper hands. So I — I, well, you see, I have my own chemistry lab in my upstairs room at home."

" So? "

" I mixed up a solution of — of mentonite."

" Of what? "

" Mentonite," Gordon repeated. " It's a clear liquid solution. Anyway, I wet a rag with it and went over to Pete's house and mopped some of it on the box. Whoever took that box is certain to have some of that solution on his hands."

" Jumpin' Jehoshaphat, boy! " Lieutenant Coleman was on his feet. " You set a trap, and you've been keeping it quiet all — "

" Say, if it's a clear solution, that — that, what did you call it? " put in Lloyd Dyer.

" Mentonite."

" If it's a clear solution, how could you see it on anyone's hands? "

" It's clear, all right," Gordon said, " and ordinarily you can't see it. But when you put it under an ultraviolet light it gives off a kind of greenish fluorescence."

Lieutenant Coleman started to reach for the button to buzz the sergeant, then hesitated. " But whoever it was who dug around in that slush and got the box last night — well, he has probably washed his hands a half-dozen times by now."

" Doesn't matter," Gordon said. " The microscopic crystals of mentonite cling for days. They practically have to wear off. Oh, there's one sure thing to remove it — or, at least, to neutralize it so it can't be detected."

" What's that? " Lloyd Dyer asked.

" Powdered gentian violet," Gordon said.

174

" Gentian violet? " Pete looked at his friend, puzzled.

" Guess you didn't know that, did you, Pete? " Gordon said. " Just a light dusting of it removes any trace of mentonite."

Pete not only didn't know it, but he had never heard of mentonite. However, when it came to chemistry, there were a lot more things he had never heard of than things he had. So he decided to keep quiet and try to look intelligent. This had become Gordon's show, anyway.

Julie said, " You mean ordinary gentian violet powder like we use in the school lab, Gordon? "

" Uh-huh," the boy nodded. " It's all the same stuff. Get it at any drugstore. But whoever got that box won't know anything about it."

It hadn't taken Lieutenant Coleman long to arrive at a decision. He pressed the buzzer furiously. Sergeant Haskins rushed in. " Sergeant," the detective instructed, " round up Zucco, Hans Oberheath — Say, we don't have an ultraviolet light here anyway," he said, turning back toward Gordon.

" The hospital probably has several of them," Gordon offered helpfully.

" Sure, that's right." Lieutenant Coleman turned again to Sergeant Haskins. " Contact Logan too. Have him bring in the guy with the gray topcoat. Book him for vagrancy — anything. And rush it, Sergeant. Things may pop here pretty quick."

Seeming to sense probably the hottest story of his career with the *Globe*, Lloyd Dyer was all eagerness. " I know where Oberheath hangs out," he volunteered. " Been kind of keeping an eye on him myself. I've got to run down to the office to file a couple of stories anyway. I'll have 'em hold the presses for a while too. I can pick up Oberheath on my way back. This might be it! "

" Yeah, yeah, O.K.," Lieutenant Coleman said. " But hurry it up. We're not going to hold up any proceedings, even for the press."

Soon the three young people and Lieutenant Coleman were alone in the office. For a couple of minutes the detective paid no attention to their presence. Pete had a strange feeling that the reason was simply that Lieutenant Coleman didn't trust what might come out if he started to talk.

Finally, though, he looked at Gordon and spoke calmly — the kind of calmness that comes only from self-discipline in a moment of excitement. " I suppose you realize," he said, " that if this is some kind of hoax — some harebrained idea of yours — that I'll turn you out to the wolves. Know what I mean? "

Gordon thought a minute. His Adam's apple bobbed up and down a couple of times. He started to say something, but couldn't seem to get the words out. He nodded that he understood.

Julie said: " Lieutenant Coleman, I don't think you give Gordon enough credit. He would never do anything like that. Would you, Gordon? "

The boy smiled — a kind of sickly smile, but the best he seemed able to muster at the moment.

All Pete could do was to look at him and wonder — wonder what was going on behind those horn-rimmed glasses that his friend was wearing — wonder if his science-minded neighbor had gone off his rocker — won-

176

der why he, Pete, hadn't stepped in and tried to save the day when there was still a chance.

For, if Pete had ever been sure of anything, he was certain right then that his friend Gordon Newhall was running the biggest hoax of his life.

And Pete felt completely helpless to do anything about it.

WHILE they sat waiting, Gordon got up, walked over to the furnace register, and opened it full on.

" Hey, it's warm enough in here," Lieutenant Coleman said. " Don't tinker around with — "

" Lieutenant Coleman," Gordon said, " we need it hot in here or — or my experiment won't work."

" Now, see here, son — "

" Please, sir," Gordon said, " just this one thing. It may be uncomfortable for a little while, but — well, if we catch the guilty person it's worth it, isn't it? "

Lieutenant Coleman shook his head in resignation. " All right," he said. " We're in this far. Guess I can go one more step. But that doesn't mean I have to keep my coat on, I guess." He slipped his coat off and hung it over the back of his chair.

" Kid," the detective said, sitting down again. " I don't know what makes me go along with you on this. But you must know something. It'd better make sense. That's all I can say. It'd better make sense! "

It was twenty minutes before a uniformed policeman led a protesting Mr. Zucco into Lieutenant Cole-

177

man's office. Shortly thereafter a plain-clothes man, whom Pete guessed to be Logan, ushered in the man with the gray topcoat. Now, with his first close look, Pete saw that he was a rather young man with straight, firm features and a muscular build that even his gray topcoat failed to hide entirely. He was not the kind of fellow Pete would want to tangle with. He protested only mildly to Lieutenant Coleman about being picked up.

Lloyd Dyer and Hans Oberheath were the last to arrive. "He gave me just a little bit of trouble," the newsman said, showing a tear on the sleeve of his jacket. "Guess I'd have been smarter if I'd let the police go after him, at that. Phew, it's hot in here!"

"Don't worry about the weather," Lieutenant Coleman said. "Just find a seat."

As soon as everyone was seated, the detective began to explain the reasons for the gathering. He spent several minutes reviewing the happenings of the past two days. Pete saw how Hans Oberheath watched Lieutenant Coleman's lips. With a little of the apparent satisfaction of being top feline in a cat-and-mouse game, the chief of detectives began to drop tiny morsels of evidence as bait to drag out various reactions. As far as Pete could make out, there seemed to be no reactions. Then Lieutenant Coleman apparently figured the time was ripe to tip over the bait bucket.

"Through a bit of rather clever amateur police work on the part of these kids," he said, "whichever one of you folks stole that tin box failed to reckon with a bit of strategy. That, of course, is assuming the guilty person is in this room — which we don't know."

"That's something to think about," Mr. Zucco said sharply.

"Well, no one will get hurt, anyway," Lieutenant Coleman said. "The guilty one — if he's smart — won't be here. However, the smarter a criminal gets, the more he leaves himself wide open. In this case, whoever stole that box last night has got his hands smeared with— with — " The detective consulted a slip of paper on his desk. "Mentonite."

Everyone — even Pete and Gordon and Julie — automatically glanced at their hands.

Lieutenant Coleman smiled. "It's not that easy," he said. "The stuff only shows up under an ultraviolet light. So, I think we may be able to wind this whole thing up in a hurry, simply by walking the short hundred yards across the park to the hospital. They have several ultraviolet lights over there, and — "

"Yeah, let's get out of here," Lloyd Dyer said, loosening his collar. "You seem determined to roast us alive. Can't you shut off that heat?"

"Lieutenant," Mr. Zucco spoke up, "what did you say was smeared on the — the carton?"

"Carton, nothing," the detective said. "It was a tin box, and acting dumb's not going to draw any water around here."

"All right, tin box," Mr. Zucco said sharply. "What did you say was smeared on it by this — this boy?"

"Mentonite. I said mentonite. You should know, since you're a chemist yourself — or are you?"

Mr. Zucco didn't answer. He scowled over at Gordon, then turned his attention back to the detective. "I've been a scientist and a chemist for nearly forty

179

years," he said. " As far as I know, there is no solution or compound called mentonite."

There was a positive way in which he said it that caused the detective to stiffen noticeably and swing around to face directly at Gordon. The challenge in his eyes was unmistakable.

" Phew," Lloyd Dyer complained, mopping at his sweaty forehead, " can't you even open a door in here? "

Lieutenant Coleman wasn't listening. He continued to stare at Gordon.

But Gordon's eyes had been attracted by something else.

" O.K., Newhall," the detective demanded in a voice that was scarcely more than a whisper, " explain to Mr. Zucco that there is such a thing as mentonite."

Gordon turned his attention back to the speaker. " Lieutenant Coleman," he said, and Pete noticed a definite quaver in his friend's voice, " I — I have a confession to make. Mr. Zucco is right. There — there isn't any such thing as mentonite — as far as I know."

" What! " Lieutenant Coleman's roar made the lights blink. " You'll go to jail for this! Sure as I'm — "

" But there is such a thing as powdered gentian violet," Gordon cut in quickly.

Pete was unable to follow the direction of Gordon's thoughts. But he could verify the gentian violet business, recalling the day he had dusted a little of it on the bare arms of several of his laboratory classmates. They hadn't even been aware of it until they had started to wash up after lab. Then the moisture had converted the microscopic particles of gentian violet dust to —

180

". . . As long as it stays dry," Gordon was explaining to Lieutenant Coleman, "you'd never detect its presence in small quantities. Like if you had dusted it on your hands lightly to neutralize the effect of — of, say, mentonite."

Lieutenant Coleman glanced back to Mr. Zucco for verification.

"He's right about the properties of gentian violet," the chemistry teacher confirmed. "It's a very strong purple dye, as well as having antiseptic qualities. When moistened, the tiniest bit — "

Lieutenant Coleman had stopped listening. He was staring straight ahead. Gordon and Julie followed his gaze. Pete heard his sister suck in her breath, and pivoted his head to see what she was looking at.

There was a long moment of agonizing silence, as Mr. Zucco's words faded out and he looked in the direction the others were staring.

All eyes had turned toward Lloyd Dyer, had focused their gaze on the splotch of deep purple that spread across his freely perspiring forehead.

A strange, puzzled fear began to creep onto the newsman's face. He looked down, and saw the telltale purple on his sweaty hands. Purple, where a few minutes earlier there had been no sign of the fine powder that he had purchased at a drugstore, and had carefully dusted on his hands to neutralize the "mentonite."

Then, even as the roomful of people watched, the realization that he had been made the unwitting victim of a hoax dawned on him. A violent fury began to erase the fear from his face.

With a shout Lloyd Dyer leaped to his feet and

181

rushed for the door.

Leaning forward in his chair, Pete was tense and ready for action. As Dyer rushed past, he launched himself forward and brought the newsman down hard with a flying tackle.

They rolled on the floor. Dyer bellowed and tried to kick away from Pete's grasp. But the young Oakmont High athlete held tight to Dyer's legs, and ducked away from the newsman's frantically flailing fists. Lieutenant Coleman and Sergeant Haskins jumped in and grabbed Lloyd Dyer. They hauled him to his feet. Pete got back up, brushing his clothes.

"Well," Lieutenant Coleman said, as Sergeant Haskins quickly slapped some handcuffs on Dyer's wrists, "that should just about wind up the calisthenics for today. Take him down and lock him up, Sergeant. He'll answer questions later. Right now there are a few items I want to get straight with these folks."

They could hear Lloyd Dyer shouting his protests right up to the moment when the metallic clank of the barred jail doors snuffed out his frantic and ineffectual dissent.

Lieutenant Coleman wiped his forehead, looked at his unstained hand, and smiled. "Newhall," he said to Gordon, "is there any reason for leaving that furnace turned up full blast now?"

"No, sir," Gordon said, pulling out of his deep thoughtfulness. "There's no need for it any longer. It — it was just the best way I knew of getting Lloyd Dyer to perspire."

"Look," the detective said, "if you figured it was Dyer all the time, why did we have to go through all this rigmarole with the Egyptian violet or — "

" Gentian violet," Gordon corrected. " I guess it does seem a little complicated, but it was the only thing I could think of at the time. You see, I have a friend who used some of the high school's supply of powder to pull a — a gag on some of the fellows in the lab one day." He smiled toward Pete, who felt pretty important right at the moment. Not only had he stopped Lloyd Dyer's attempted getaway, but now it looked as though Gordon even had copied the idea for Dyer's self-exposure from him.

" But you had a pretty good idea that Dyer was the guilty one," Lieutenant Coleman said. " After all, he was the only one here in the office when you explained that business about the — the mentonite and that violet stuff."

" Yes, sir," Gordon admitted, " I had a good idea."

" Then why didn't you just tell me? " Lieutenant Coleman demanded.

" I was afraid that if there wasn't enough proof, and if Mr. Dyer got wind that he was being suspected, he might destroy the tin box and whatever is inside of it."

" Well, that figures," Coleman admitted. " But just when did you decide that Lloyd Dyer was behind this thing? "

" Just this morning," Gordon said. " Well, really, I began to wonder yesterday — when Pete said Mr. Dyer had remarked about this being your first murder case in a long time."

" When was that? " the detective asked.

" It was when you first arrived at school the other night," Pete offered, picking up the thread of Gordon's thought. " We were all going upstairs, and Lloyd Dyer began to ask me questions. You kind of cut him short, told him that you'd ask the questions. He winked at me and said something about how he mustn't crab your act, that it was the first murder you'd had to play around with for a long time."

" Dyer said that? "

" It sounded strange when Pete mentioned it to me yesterday," Gordon said. " No one had mentioned anything about murder to you, or any of the policemen. Not up to that time. I had reasons to think it might be. I had even mentioned my suspicions to Pete and Julie."

" It hardly registered, though," Julie spoke up. " I think we were all too frightened and shocked. Those were pretty terrible minutes right after the explosion. I'm still not sure just what took place."

" Anyway," Gordon said, " just before Pete went down to Mr. Walker's office to phone, I mentioned I thought it was murder. Pete objected. I figured he probably didn't mention it over the phone. Then, when Sergeant Haskins told of his habit of jotting down his phone calls as he takes them, it made a perfect check." Gordon pulled the piece of crumpled yellow scratch paper out of his pocket. " There's no mention of murder here."

" So that made it Lloyd Dyer's idea, huh? " Lieutenant Coleman said.

" I guess something like that. At least, he was the first one to mention it. You don't usually call a thing by such a strong name as murder before you've even had a chance to see the evidence or talk to someone."

" Well, we've got Dyer," Lieutenant Coleman said.

184

" That's the part I'm particularly concerned with. But we haven't the box or its contents."

" If you'll pardon me — " The man in the gray top-coat, which he had removed in deference to the over-heated room, stepped up to Lieutenant Coleman and flipped open a wallet. The detective studied it a moment, then looked up, smiling.

" Folks," he said, " meet Carlton Spencer, Federal Bureau of Investigation."

Pete watched the mouths drop open, knowing his had also.

" This comes as a surprise to me too," Lieutenant Coleman said.

The FBI man smiled. " I guess my being here gives you the idea that Professor Nordland's work went beyond that of teaching high school science courses."

" I — I was never sure." Mr. Zucco spoke up for the first time since Lloyd Dyer's exposure. " But I some-times wondered. I know it's not uncommon, doing part-time outside research. Nordland was a quiet man. We never got along too well together. I must confess also that I began to have suspicions that his extra research efforts might not be to the American public's best in-terest."

" Allow me to set your mind at ease on that score, sir," Mr. Spencer said. " Although I cannot give you any hint as to the exact type of work he was doing, I can tell you this, since you've probably already guessed it anyway: Professor Nordland's research was of suf-ficient importance to be of definite value to certain for-eign interests, who are willing to pay rather hand-somely for such information. Unfortunately, there are

185

still a few so-called Americans circulating around who are after that kind of money."

" But Dyer," Lieutenant Coleman said, shaking his head as though finding it difficult to believe that the congenial newspaperman could be mixed up in such a vicious business.

" We've had a file on Dyer for some time," the FBI agent said. " Perhaps you recall the Midland airplane disaster last year. I don't believe we'll have too much trouble connecting Dyer with it. Not now. He has nothing to lose. As I say, we've had some suspicions of him, but no real evidence. As a matter of fact, we began to think we might have been wrong about him — until this business at Oakmont High."

" He was a pretty smooth worker, all right," Lieutenant Coleman said. " I guess we've got these kids to thank for some real help."

Carlton Spencer turned to Gordon. " That was a very nice bit of police work, son," he complimented. " The way things happened so fast, I don't suppose you had much choice. Also we must allow for the way a young mind works. But I strongly advise that in the future you go to the police first, then start working from there."

" Yes, sir," Gordon said. " And if things hadn't snowballed so fast, we sure would have this time. But it was so important to me that I shouldn't let Professor Nordland down. That tin box — " Gordon stopped suddenly. " We still haven't got the tin box or its contents."

" I think I could almost lead you to it," Carlton Spencer said, not seeming a bit worried. " Fellows like Dyer have a definite pattern to their operations. Almost a monotonous pattern, although they think they're very clever. Dyer lives alone in a rooming house. His main possession and pride is his car. Simple arithmetic would indicate that the box will be hidden someplace in the car. Logically in the trunk, or stuffed in behind the upholstery. Don't worry — we'll find the box, or at least the contents. Well, I guess that about clears up my part. Oh, yes," he tured to Gordon, " I don't suppose ' *The birches are mixed with the beeches* ' means anything in particular to you? "

Gordon stiffened as though he had been touched with a hot poker. " The — the password! " he said. " Professor Nordland instructed me to — Say, then you're the one who is supposed to get the tin box."

" That's right," Carlton Spencer said, smiling. " And if you'll excuse me, I think I'll go out to Dyer's automobile, and see how good my hunches are working today. I'll be back."

" Well," Lieutenant Coleman said, " there's no need of your sticking around, Mr. Zucco. Sorry for the inconvenience, but these things come up, you know. The person who's innocent need never worry."

" Oh, I wasn't worried," the science teacher said. " Just a bit irked, I suppose. But I'll feel better soon. I understand that I'll have the pleasure of giving Mr. Rogers here a past-due chemistry examination within the next couple of days. I will be looking forward eagerly to that event."

Pete felt the blood rush from his cheeks at the dismal thought of what Mr. Zucco could do to him by way of an examination.

But, as the stocky man left the room, he paused long

enough in the doorway to wink back at the young people. Pete felt a little better for the ray of hope the friendly gesture gave him.

Hans Oberheath was the next to leave. He seemed sufficiently anxious, although his eyes gleamed over the excitement of the past few minutes.

" I guess that about finishes it for the time being," Lieutenant Coleman said to the three young people. " Of course, you'll be called on to appear in court, and — "

" We'll be glad to do anything we can," Gordon said. " At least, I will."

" Look, pal," Pete said, " you've been doing most of the talking for Julie and me during the past couple of days. You might just as well keep it up. After all, who are we, but — "

" Pete! Gordon! " Julie exclaimed excitedly. " Look! "

Carlton Spencer came into the room carrying the dark-green tin box that had been the cause of so much trouble — including a murder — during the past two days.

" Just about where I figured," he said, smiling. " Only Dyer had a slight switch. He had fastened it with tape and wire up under the dashboard."

" Well, I guess that really winds things up," Pete said in great relief.

" Oh, there are a few loose ends," the FBI agent said. " Nothing too important. Now I guess you'll have to excuse me. It's time I made a call to my superiors. Once again, I'd like to say that you are all to be complimented on a fast and speedy job of justice. I deeply

188

regret the loss of such a fine man as Professor Nordland. It might be some comfort to you young people to know that his work has lost none of its value, and that his greatness as a scientist and loyal American will be remembered through his work." Mr. Spencer tapped the tin box by way of explaining his meaning.

Gordon, Pete, and Julie looked at each other. All three of them seemed to have been struck by the same idea.

" Let's go, Gordon," Pete suggested.

" Yeah," Gordon agreed.

Julie already had started toward the door.

" What's the hurry, kids? " Lieutenant Coleman asked.

" She'll want to know," Julie said. " She'll want to know a lot of things."

" And we've got them to tell her," Pete said.

" Tell who? "

" Mrs. Nordland," Gordon called back over his shoulder.

The three of them walked out of the police station. They paused on the steps a moment to inhale deeply of the crisp winter air. Then they walked briskly off across the park toward Mrs. Nordland's.

Biography of Charles Coombs

Charles Coombs is a six-foot-three redhead who subscribes to the old bromide that he would rather write than eat . . . a fact which came in rather handy during his first years of much writing and little eating.

An English major and a graduate of the University of California at Los Angeles, Mr. Coombs says that his class papers were often too straightforwardly adventurous in style and content to appeal to the more astute minds of the professors of literature. Yet, he managed to squeak through UCLA, receiving his Bachelor of Arts degree in 1939. With the ink scarcely dry on the sheepskin, he married a pretty classmate named Eleanor and settled down to the new duty of breadwinner.

Store clerking, carpentering, aircraft building and various odd jobs furnished meat for the table. But each job only strengthened his nearly lifelong ambition to become a writer. He set up a card table in a closet. Sitting in the doorway he pecked away at the typewriter early mornings and late nights. In 1940 he came through with a five-dollar sale to the back pages of a western magazine. The sale coincided with the birth of his first son, Lee.

Having somewhat of a background in school athletics, Mr. Coombs began writing sports stories. He enjoyed moderate success in this field until World War II created a great shortage of pulp paper. Scouting a new outlet he tried the field of juveniles.

190

"I made no great changes in style or content," he said. "Editors of youth publications seemed fed up with the wishy-washy juvenile stories of yesteryear. Both publishers and readers welcomed tales of high adventure, as long as they stayed within the limits of wholesome good taste. A straightforward style was particularly welcome."

By the end of World War II a second son, Dan, and about a hundred fiction sales were to the credit of the Coombs family. A conference was held, resulting in a family agreement that the author would give up his job and try a year of full-time writing to determine whether or not he could support his family in the highly competitive field of writing. By this time nearly ninety-per cent of his typewriter's output was aimed at the juvenile field.

The trial year resulted in around 120 consecutive fiction sales, plus an unexpected but welcome plum of becoming a Hollywood Studio Press Correspondent, which gave him "open sesame" to movie and television facilities. He now conducts motion picture and television review columns for several youth and adult magazines.

In 1946 a third child, a daughter, Lynn, made it possible to install a larger breadbox in the Coombs kitchen. Mr. Coombs added photography to his interests. Armed with camera and tripod, he began covering soaring contests, mountain climbing expeditions, anything and everything of an adventuresome nature. These jaunts resulted in pictures, articles, and much interesting background information on which to hang fiction plots.

191

"I try to work from various angles," he said, "since a scattering of effort and an attempt to acquire versatility seems fairly essential to supporting a family on writing alone."

So with a growing list of books, fiction sales, articles and columns, Mr. Coombs manages to keep a loaf of wholewheat in the breadbox, a pair of shoes on each youngster, and an occasional sparerib on the barbecue grill in the back yard of their Los Angeles home.